KATIE PATTERSON

D1522811

RIDE

outskirts
press

*This book is dedicated to my grandpa, Bill Reid,
for pushing me to pursue my dreams.*

*And to everyone else who has supported that girl
who decided she wanted to be a writer.*

I love you all.

CHAPTER 1

The roar of the incoming airplane screams above me as I walk through the sliding glass doors of the small airport. Twilight is slowly creeping into the once blue sky, and an orange glow is becoming much more defined above me. Around me, people hustle and bustle, entering or leaving the hub, talking on the phone, carrying bags, or just quickly moving.

I move against the clear glass windows away from the door. I set my two overstuffed suitcases beside me and lean up against the window, trying to act casual. When I look up at the time on the nearby clock, it reads 8:48. He's three minutes late. I reach into my designer handbag, looking for my phone, but then sadly remember it is not there, and it won't be there for another month.

I sigh and watch the line of cars pull into the pickup zone. A young man greets his wife, and I see his children running into the arms of their father. They all are so happy to see each other, excited for what is to come. They have been looking forward to his arrival all week. Me, I have been dreading mine.

Finally, a gray Mercedes pulls up. The driver parks the car and opens the door.

"Alyson!" My grandpa beams, stepping out of the car.

"Hello…" I say, putting a smile on my face.

"Sorry I'm late," he says. "There was a bit of construction on the highway that slowed me down."

"It's okay. It was only ten minutes."

He grabs my bags and opens the trunk. Fortunately, the car is an SUV, because if it were any smaller my bags wouldn't fit. He loads everything into the car while I hop into the passenger seat.

He jumps in the driver's seat beside me, and starts the engine. The car gives a small rumble as it starts up, and then the engine instantly roars to life. He exits the loading zone. I don't even look back at the small airport.

As we get on the two-lane highway, I cannot help but look up at the sky. For several minutes, the two of us just watch the fiery orange and red swirls come across the horizon. The whole sky above me seems to glow in a welcoming way. It's as if we are driving beneath a painting. This is something I don't ever see in Los Angeles.

My grandpa looks over at me. "How was your flight?" he asks.

"Fine," I say looking straight ahead.

"And did your connection in Colorado leave smoothly?"

I nod.

"And did you enjoy the last semester of your junior year?"

"I guess," I say, not even attempting to keep the conversation going.

"How were your grades?"

"All A's," I plainly state.

"Excellent." He smiles. "We will have to celebrate."

"At least someone seems to appreciate them," I say.

"Your parents were not thrilled?"

"Let's just say they were kind of preoccupied with other things."

"Oh, I see. Well, are you looking forward to being here? Because I know your grandma and I are."

I shrug. "It was kind of last minute, but I guess."

My grandpa looks hurt by what I have said.

"That's not what I meant," I quickly say. "I meant more like it was so last minute I haven't had enough time to fully grasp the idea. The lake will be nice though..."

He nods. "I can understand. Is there anything in particular you want to do during your visit?"

"I don't know," I reply.

"Well, we have a boat, Jet Skis, and an assortment of tubes and various water toys."

"Okay, sounds cool." I lean my head up against the side of the car.

"Are you tired?" he asks.

"A little."

"Well, we have about a two-hour drive to the cottage. Feel free to sleep. I will wake you up when we get there."

"Okay." I close my eyes and let my mind begin to wander. Why did I even have to come here? But I don't pity myself for long because I know I want nothing more than to be back in Los Angeles, California, going to beach parties, shopping with my friends, using electronics. Besides, all the best events happen during the summer. I want to have the perfect summer before senior year, but from the looks of things, spending my summer in a small lake town won't be up to the standards I was hoping for.

I think back to the day my parents decided to send me here. I can see them yelling at me, standing in the foyer of the large white house. I see my mom in her high heels and fancy necklace, confronting me about what I did. I see myself trying to come up with another lie, but she knows too much. My parents said I was out of control and that I needed to get my act together.

It was then that they decided that spending the summer with my grandparents would be the best choice. Of course I disagreed, and I still do. My parents just don't understand my motives. They don't understand my life.

My mom is a former model. At the height of her career, she was modeling for major designer brands. She still does some work with various companies, but she now works as a spokesperson for the fashion department of a popular magazine.

My dad is also in the "Hollywood glam" business. He works as a producer for a successful movie company. He mostly does Indie films for film festivals, but he has managed to make a name for himself. One of the films he produced won best short film one year, and he is currently working on the next "blockbuster" supposedly.

I guess my parents have pretty cool jobs, and many people say I have really cool parents, but a lot of people do not understand the price that comes with great jobs.

Still awake, I direct my attention to the music playing in the car.

It is a CD because I remember seeing Track 1 appear on the console when I got in. Even though the music has been playing this whole time, I'm just beginning to take notice. The melody is calm and soothing. I think many people, like my mom, would classify it as "depressing," but I find it to be the exact opposite. The music makes me feel relaxed. It makes everything around me feel so real.

I begin to focus in on the lyrics, about someone who feels inadequate, a failure. Their fall from grace. Those lyrics stand out to me the most as I continue to think of my life and how this is going to be the worst month of it. I fall asleep just wanting to go home.

———((•))———

I am jolted awake when I feel the car shift from the smooth paved road to a gravelly dirt one. I can hear the rocks and pebbles crack and shake under the road. Very welcoming. I sit up and rub my eyes before looking at the clock. It reads 10:50 p.m. "We're almost there," I hear my grandpa tell me, "just around the corner."

I look out the window into the pitch black. When I can't see anything, I direct my attention out the front window. In the headlights' path, I can see the narrow dirt road. On one side of me there is a lush, heavily wooded forest. On the other side, I see the shadows of various homes.

Finally, we turn onto a paved driveway. My grandpa stops the car and I open my door. I step out into the night and look up at the sky. Above me, hundreds and hundreds of twinkling stars shine bright. The whole sky seems to be a mixture of dark navy and a bright, miraculous silver that appears to stretch on for miles. This is definitely not the smoggy, bleached sky at home.

I close my door and instantly feel the cool breeze on my face. It sends a shiver up my spine, and I can't help but cross my arms and try to stay warm in my leather jacket and jeans. I smell the fresh scent of the rolling green grass, and I hear the welcoming chirp of the crickets. The sound of the lake's waves is peaceful as they lap up onto the shore from behind the house.

Though it is hard to see the house in the dark, I manage to make out the whitewashed cottage in front of me. It's a good size, with screened-in windows and emerald-green shutters. It even has a large porch on the side of the house. Across from the house, and next to the car, I notice a large four-car garage that matches the cottage.

My grandpa walks around to the trunk and begins to unload my luggage. I grab my purse and begin to walk to the screened-in door. Right then, I see the door swing open and my grandma come out.

"Alyson!" She beams. "Look at you!"

"Hi," I say, climbing the wooden porch steps and giving her a hug.

She puts her arm around me and escorts me into the home. "How was your flight?"

"Okay," I reply as I'm led into a small entrance hallway with wood paneling on the lower half of the wall and plain white paint on the upper half. In the hallway, there are two doorways, each branching off into various rooms. I slip off my shoes and follow my grandma through the door opening into the kitchen.

The kitchen is modern and updated with stainless steel appliances, granite countertops, and light wooden cabinetry. On the fridge, I notice dozens of pictures of family and friends of my grandparents. I even see some with me and my brothers and sister.

The kitchen leads into an open living room with a stone fireplace and more wood-paneled walls. Ivy-green comfy-looking couches sit in the room, and a rustic chandelier completes the scene. Off to the side of the room is a long, narrow dining room table that looks as if it can hold sixteen people. In the living room are two sets of glass double doors, and I quickly glance out at the dark moonlit lake.

"I haven't seen you in so long!" my grandma says, standing behind me.

"I know," I reply. "I think I was like thirteen or something."

"And look at you now! You're a senior in high school!"

I smile. "This is a nice place you have. It is weird I have never been here before."

"Well, your parents were very busy when you were young."

"They still are..."

"Let me take you upstairs."

Silently, I follow her. Upstairs, I find five rooms, one already occupied by my grandparents. Two of the rooms have queen beds, one has two twins, and the last one has bunk beds. I choose a lake-facing room with a queen bed. The room is way smaller than the one I have at home, but I decide I will have to make it work.

My grandpa brings me my bags, and the three of us stand in the room silently. Finally my grandma looks up at me. "Your grandpa and I are both so happy you could come visit us this summer!"

I put a smile on my face, not knowing how to reply, because in all honesty I want nothing more than to go home.

"What do you normally do during the summers?" my grandpa asks, trying to keep the conversation going.

"Normally my family travels, or I hang out with friends, but it doesn't look like I will be doing either of those things this summer." At this point, I couldn't care less about pleasing my grandparents. The reality of not being home is starting to set in, and this strange place is making me feel uneasy. Not to mention, I haven't seen my grandparents in years.

My grandpa looks slightly upset. "Well, is there anything you want to do while you're here?"

Even though I already answered this question, I decide to answer it a little differently. "Yes, actually I want to go back to California." I pause. They both just look at me. "I'm sorry. I'm tired. Can I go to bed?"

"You may," my grandpa says, "but let me say something first. You have made it very clear since the moment you got in the car that you would like to be home, but we cannot make that happen. We want to please you this summer, but your request is out of our hands, so please try to have a better attitude. This is new for all of us."

"It's not like you want me here either. You didn't even know I was coming until last week when my parents asked you to 'babysit' me," I say, sitting down on the bed.

"Yes, but we have been looking forward to your arrival since we received the news."

"Really, because last time I checked, I haven't seen you in years." I take a deep breath. "Thank you for picking me up. I think I'll be going to bed now."

Once alone in my room, I pull the wooden chair from my desk and prop it up against my window. I open up the shutters and let the cool air seep into the room. I sit in the chair and stare out into the night. Since my room faces the lake, I can't help but admire the glossy moonlit water. Its purple waters sway back and forth in the breeze, and I am instantly mesmerized by the oscillation of the small waves.

After I have watched the water long enough, I bury my head in my hands and let tears run down my eyes. What did I do back there? I just ruined any chance of connecting with my grandparents. Now they probably think I am some snotty, rich, selfish kid.

I take a deep breath. While I do have to accept the fact I am here, in Minnesota, I just can't. I mean, I guess I kind of want to see my grandparents, but I would rather be home where I belong. It is here, looking out onto the lake, that I decide I will fight until my parents allow me to come home.

I begin to unpack my clothes from the two large suitcases, figuring I should at least look like I made an effort to be at home here. I carefully fold some of the frilly shirts and trendy tank tops into the wooden dresser. I unfold my designer jeans and shorts and place them in the drawer as well. I hang up all my gorgeous summer dresses and garish skirts in the closet. Finally, I place all my makeup and perfume on top of the dresser. I look at the boring green bedding and place a small worn-out teddy bear on it. I look around and admire the work I have done. I smile. This will do for the short time I'm here.

The last thing in my suitcase is a white cardboard box wrapped in a plastic bag. I take one look at the small box and zip the suitcase closed. I don't want to look at that box ever again. I push the now almost empty suitcases into the closet and close the door.

I drift off to sleep on top of the covers, listening to the waves lap the shore of the lake.

CHAPTER 2

I wake up to a voice calling my name. "Alyson, Alyson," my grandma says in a soft voice.

"What?" I moan, rolling over toward her.

"It is time to get up!" she says, sounding cheery.

I rub my eyes and squint at the clock through blurred vision. It reads 7:02.

"It's too early," I say as I roll over again and pull the covers closer to my body. Someone must have tucked me in last night.

"Well, your parents specifically told me that you should be up at seven o'clock sharp every morning. That way you avoid staying up too late and getting up too late."

I groan. "I don't want to."

"Yes, you do," my grandma replies. "I expect you to be downstairs in fifteen minutes."

I sit up. "Grandma, can I talk to you for a minute?"

She nods.

"I just want to say I am sorry for the way I acted last night. I was just overwhelmed and I guess I took my anger out on you. I'm excited to see you and Grandpa, but I wish it was not in a way like this. I'm just upset with the situation."

"Don't worry about it." She smiles. "This is a difficult time in your life, and I can see how you could be conflicted. We want to help you in any way we can so when you do go home, you can decide how you want to live your life. Anyway, I see you got unpacked."

I nod.

"And don't worry, you're not in trouble here." She smiles. "This is a hard transition for both of us, but especially for you. I know what you are going through seems unfair and wrong, and I know you don't like it, but I am always here for you. I am always ready to talk."

"Thank you."

"I will let you get ready. After all, it is rather late." She winks.

"Thanks," I say again, and she smiles at me.

"Oh, and one more thing!" My grandma bends down and picks up a cardboard box, which she sets on my bed. "In here are clothes that your mother used to wear when she was up here. I bet they would fit you, and they are not that out of style. They are just some basic shirts, if you want to wear them, in case you find your clothes are a little much for around here." She chuckles.

"Thanks, but I am sure my clothes will be fine."

"Keep them anyway."

"Will do."

"See you downstairs," she says.

"Oh, and Grandma?" I call after her.

She looks back.

"Does anyone know why I'm here?"

She shakes her head.

"Well, if they ask, can you please tell them I'm just here for a regular old vacation?"

"Alyson, in our eyes you are."

I smile as she leaves.

I lie in bed, looking up at the plain white ceiling, trying to find the will to get up, but I can't. Not only did my parents send me half-way across the country to some little town, they also decided I have to get an early wake-up call.

When I finally manage to sit up again, I realize that I left my window open all night. I now hear the birds singing their morning songs and the slight breeze rustling the tree limbs outside my window. I can hear the water lapping against the shore. I push the covers away and slide out of bed onto the light wooden floor. I stretch in the sunrays that beam through my window, and walk over to the mirror hanging on the wall.

I take one look at my long, messy brown hair and groan. I brush it, and put it in a ponytail. Then I go through my daily makeup routine, making sure my eyes have the perfect balance of eyeliner and mascara. I put on a simple floral skirt and pink top. This outfit should be casual enough.

Downstairs, my grandma is in the kitchen making breakfast, but she doesn't acknowledge me. My grandpa is not in the room.

The house, with its many windows, is brightly lit. The fresh morning air seeps in through the windows. I take a look around the empty living room and decide to go outside. I open the screen door and step out onto a stone slab patio. The door clicks shut behind me, and I walk out a couple of feet before turning around to look at the house.

It is much easier to see it in the daytime. Its white wooden structure stands out even more than it did last night, and this time I notice the stone fireplace outline that runs between the two sets of glass doors.

My grandma has nicely arranged patio furniture on the stone deck. On the grass I see various inner tubes pushed up against the house, and a clothesline with beach towels hanging between two trees in the yard.

It's then that I finally see the long, plastic white dock. Four colorful beach chairs are lined up in a perfect row across its surface. Off to one side, my grandpa's boat sits in its lift, and on the other side I see two tethered Jet Skis.

I squint, looking past the dock where the water spreads out across the shimmering lake. I can barely see the land on the other side. This lake isn't big, but it isn't small either.

"Never seen a body of water before?" I hear a voice call to me.

I look over to my right and see a girl, about my age. She has wavy blonde hair that falls past her shoulders and blue eyes. She's very tan. She wears a white shirt, which hangs gently over one shoulder, and denim shorts. She holds a stack of towels in her hand.

"Actually, I live by the ocean," I reply, not knowing how else to respond.

"Well, it looked like you were enchanted by the lake."

"Oh," I say.

"I'm just kidding!" She smiles. She sets the towels down on a chair and crosses through the trees over to my yard. "I'm Chloe Coleman," she says, holding out her hand.

I shake it. "Alyson Butler."

"You must be the Henderbells' granddaughter! We have all heard about your arrival!"

"You have?"

"Yeah! Everyone is really excited to meet you."

"Oh."

"Anyway, I live next door. Well, technically I live in Minneapolis, but I spend my summers here with my grandparents."

"Nice," I say. "I'm from California."

"So I have heard!" Chloe smiles. She pauses. "So are you and your grandma going somewhere fancy today?" She looks at my skirt and shirt.

"No, I don't think so. Why do you ask?" I say, confused.

"Well, you are all dressed up."

"Oh, this... I just tried to find something...basic." I look at Chloe's casual dress and suddenly I feel awkward. Back at home, what I am wearing now would be considered very casual and fun.

"Anyway," Chloe changes the subject, "I have to hang up these towels on the line, but we should hang out sometime!"

"Yeah," I say. "I know absolutely no one here."

"Just you wait!" She laughs. "If I don't see you before, I will see you at the barbeque tomorrow."

"Barbeque?"

"Yeah, the weekly neighborhood one. They are really fun! Your grandma always prepares the best food!"

"Oh," I say again, beginning to realize there's a lot more to this town than I originally thought.

"Well, see you around, Alyson!"

"Bye, Chloe," I say, watching her skip back into her yard.

I turn back toward the house and see my grandma standing in

the doorway. "I see you have met Chloe," she says. "She is such a nice young lady."

"Yeah," I reply.

"Breakfast is on the table. Eat up. When you are done, I want you to come into town with me so I can show you around. Then you can spend the rest of the day by the lake."

"Okay." I begin to walk to the table. All I wanted to do today was lie in the sun and use the phone to call some friends; but apparently that won't be happening. My so-called vacation is beginning to look like a family event.

The town of Davis Lake, Minnesota, basically consists of one large main drag and various other streets with small homes. It is on the opposite side of the lake from my grandparents' home, about a ten-minute drive. Honestly, I am surprised people can actually live in such a small town. I mean, where do people shop and go out to dinner?

The main street is lined with sections of one-story buildings with white facades. I see a bank, a post office, hardware store, ice cream shop, and a restaurant called Juliet's Bistro. I also take notice of several other shops specializing in antiques and sewing. Each shop has a striped covering above its large display windows, and pots of flowers outside.

My grandma continues to the end of the main street toward the edge of town. I look out the window, taking in my surroundings, trying to find anything fun to help pass the time here.

Finally, she pulls up to a small building called Paul's Grocery.

"I just need to pick up a few ingredients for the barbeque tomorrow. It won't take long. If you like, you can walk up the street and take a look at the town. Here is some money if you want to get something to eat or drink."

"Okay, thank you," I say, taking the money.

"I will meet you back here in, let's say, fifteen minutes?"

"Sounds good."

She goes into the store and I begin to walk up the street. As I walk, I notice people looking at my outfit. The more I look around at the casual shorts and normal T-shirts, the more overdressed I feel. This makes me long even more for LA, because at home I would be complimented instead of judged.

Toward the top of the street, there is a convenience store. I walk in and buy a water bottle and the new edition of a fashion magazine. Maybe I can somewhat keep up with the trends. Seeing I have time left before I have to meet my grandma, I decide to walk to the edge of the lake and look at the clear water. It ripples gently, and when I look at it, I can see my reflection.

I then decide to walk back to the store to meet my grandma. I look down at the magazine and begin to read the headlines when I hear loud voices in front of me. I look up to see three teenagers running down the street toward me. The first one passes me, and so does the second, but the third trips on the uneven ground and falls right into me, knocking my water from my hands. I try to jump back, but it all happens so fast and the water splashes onto my skirt and legs as it hits the hard pavement.

Stepping back and trying to shake the water from my wet hands, I look at him. He, too, steps back. He has deep blue eyes and golden brown hair that sweeps gently over his eyebrows. "I'm... I'm...so sorry..." he says, looking down at the spilled water, looking mortified.

I just look at him, not sure how to respond.

"Sorry!" he says again, looking into my eyes. I can't tell if he means it or not.

"Hey!" One of the other boys with dark hair laughs. "Let's go!"

He looks back at me and follows his two friends again as they laugh, leaving me dripping wet from my waist down.

———— ◈ ————

I spend the rest of the day in the sun lying on the dock. The sun's rays are radiant and direct, and I know I will get a good tan. My grandpa decides to play music from the sixties and seventies from his boat while he cleans it in the water. Normally the old music would annoy me, but in a way I find it comforting.

I think back to California. I think of my friends, who are probably either at the beach or the mall, and my family, who is probably not minding my absence.

A little while later, I decide to go up to the house to get something to drink. I slip my swim cover-up over my swimsuit and walk up the grassy hill toward the white cottage.

I slide through the screen door and into the living room. I walk to the kitchen and open the fridge. I see a pitcher of lemonade and pour myself a glass. Then I stand, alone, in the kitchen, silently sipping my beverage. It is then that I hear the familiar voice of my grandma in the other room. "You do not need to worry, Alyssa. She is fine, just fine. Still getting settled in, but your father and I have no concerns."

Great, I think. Even here, my mom doesn't trust me.

"Yes, I will keep you updated. Please do not worry."

My grandma hangs up and walks into the kitchen. "I see you finally came in."

I nod, continuing to sip the lemonade. "Who were you on the phone with?" I ask, already knowing the answer.

"I was talking to your mother actually," she says.

"Does she think I've done something bad already?" I ask in an annoyed tone.

"No, she just wanted to make sure you got here okay."

"Of course she did," I dully reply.

The kitchen falls silent. My grandma walks over to the fridge to pour herself some lemonade.

"Alyson," she says after a while, "I am going over to a neighbor's home for a little bit to drop some food off. If you would like, you can join me."

Seeing I have nothing else to do, I say yes.

I run upstairs to get dressed. In my room I quickly pull open one of my drawers of clothes and dig through, looking for something very casual to wear. After my outfit today, I need something toned down. I find a pair of simple white shorts, but all of my shirts seem to be a little too much for going to the neighbor's house. I sigh, contemplating what to do. Then I remember the box of clothes my grandma gave me. I walk over to the closet where I stored the box and drag it to the middle of the room.

I tear off the duct-taped seal and begin to dig through the old cardboard box. My grandma was right. These clothes are too plain to be out of style. I see simple T-shirts and blouses, along with various sweatshirts and sweaters. I pick a simple light blue denim button-up shirt to wear and run a brush through my tangled hair before rejoining my grandma back downstairs.

"I like your shirt." She winks at me as she sets various bags on the granite counter.

I smile back.

"Alyson, if you don't mind, could you help me carry these to the car?"

"Of course," I reply.

We each take a handful and exit the house. My grandma opens the car's trunk and I begin to load the bags into the back. "Why are you taking so many groceries to your neighbors?" I ask as I load the last two bags.

"Well," she says, closing the trunk and getting into the car, "there is an old man named Mr. Bennett who lives down the street. He is such a kind man, but he is too old to drive himself anywhere, so everyone on our street takes turns helping him out and bringing him what he needs."

"Oh, that's nice." I smile.

"I wanted to bring you along because he has always wanted to meet you."

"He knows who I am?"

"Well, let's just say I do a lot of work there, and he enjoys hearing about my grandchildren. He tells me he always wanted kids, but his wife passed away when they were both young, and he never remarried."

"Oh," I say, not sure how to respond.

"Anyway, you can help me put the groceries away and prepare him some dinner."

"Sounds good."

The car ride only lasts a minute and then we are pulling up to a small, old, one-story home. It has fresh-looking light green paint and white trim. It even has a luscious garden and picket fence.

"Did you guys do all this?"

My grandma nods.

She stops the car in the gravel driveway and walks over to the trunk. I follow too, but I then notice a new-looking black Range Rover in the driveway.

"Grandma?" I ask, confused. "Why does Mr. Bennett have a car if he can't drive?"

My grandma looks over. "Oh, that car belongs to Marc Maylore, who lives down the street. He is always here helping when he can. He is such a caring and considerate young man."

I grab some grocery bags and follow my grandma toward the home.

"Knock, knock!" my grandma calls as she enters the screened door on the side of the house. I follow her into a small dark entry hall. I can make out the door to a bedroom and bath, and I see the kitchen at the end of the hall. On the other side of the home is a long living room with a porch. The house smells of cookies and men's cologne, and all the furniture looks like it has come right out of the sixties. Even the TV looks decades old.

My grandma leads me into the back of the living room onto a screened-in porch that overlooks the lake. I can make out the back of a man sitting in an armchair.

"Timothy," my grandma calls, "there is someone I would like you to meet."

He turns around and smiles. "You must be Alyson." He beams, extending an old wrinkly hand.

I nod and shake it. "It's a pleasure to meet you, Mr. Bennett."

"Oh, no need to call me Mr. Bennett. Tim is completely acceptable."

"I like Mr. Bennett." I laugh.

He smiles. For an old man in his late eighties, Mr. Bennett looks very good. Though his skin is wrinkly and his body looks old, his green eyes and smile look very young. He has even taken the effort to put himself together, combing his snow-white hair back and wearing a button-up shirt with slacks and dark suspenders.

"You have grown into quite the young lady. I remember seeing pictures of you when you were only a little girl. How old are you now?"

"Thank you, and I'm seventeen."

"Well, you are becoming quite the young lady then."

"I guess you could say that," I say, wishing his statement were true.

"Alyson, go place those bags in the kitchen, and Marc will help you put them away. Then you and Mr. Bennett will have plenty of time to chat," my grandma says.

"Okay." I enter the dark hallway to go to the kitchen.

Even though I still have negative feelings toward this small town in Minnesota, I decide that since I'm finally beginning to meet people, I need to appear to have a better attitude. I need to be excited, happy, and thoughtful. I need to act like I'm on a vacation, and I will first show this new kindhearted spirit when I introduce myself to this Marc guy.

I'm not surprised when I walk into an outdated kitchen. It is well kept up though, with light cabinetry and a laminate countertop. At first I think the kitchen is empty, but when I look closer, I notice the figure behind the refrigerator door, looking for something.

Deciding to introduce myself in a confident voice, I say, "Hi you must be Marc. I'm..." But then I stop midsentence because Marc looks up from the fridge, and right in front of me stands the guy with the golden brown hair and deep blue eyes who spilled water all over me.

"You're Mrs. Henderbell's granddaughter?" Marc looks at me with a shocked face.

"And you're Marc Maylore, the guy who in the last five minutes, my grandma has talked so highly of?" I am pretty sure I look just as surprised as he does.

His face turns bright red. "Let me just say I had no clue who you were..."

"So? Are you saying that it is all right to spill water on someone, and run away laughing whether you know them or not?"

"No, no, not at all, it's just..."

"It's just what?"

He looks at me with a blank expression.

"I see..." I say in an annoyed voice. How could someone be so rude to me?

"No. No, you don't understand. I'm so sorry," he says.

I set the bags on the counter and quickly exit the kitchen.

"Wait!" Marc calls, following me out. "I didn't get your name."

"It doesn't matter!" I say, raising my voice as I move down the hall. "And if you don't mind, I think I will be leaving now!" By now, my voice is at a yell. I exit through the front door, slamming it behind me, and leaving Marc, Mr. Bennett, and my grandma standing in the hall watching me go.

CHAPTER 3

My grandma never asks me about my overly dramatic exit at Mr. Bennett's house. I assume that is because either Marc told her or she decided to leave the subject alone.

That evening after dinner I decide to be polite and help my grandma with the dishes when I hear a knock on the door. "Come in!" my grandma calls, not even bothering to see who it is.

I give her a weird look.

"Don't worry, Alyson, it is just a neighbor. Always is."

I hear the door swing open and closed, and then Chloe from next door enters the kitchen. "Hello, Mrs. Henderbell," she pauses and looks my way, "Alyson."

"Hello, Chloe," my grandma replies. I give a friendly nod. "What can I do for you?"

"Well, I was wondering if Alyson wanted to bike up the road and watch the sunset by the creek. I thought she might enjoy it on her first full night here."

Quickly I decide to say yes. I guess it could be cool, and getting to know Chloe, the only other girl my age around here, might be a good idea. I open my mouth to respond, but my grandma says something instead.

"Thank you for the lovely offer, but Alyson is not allowed to leave the house after nine, and it is 8:45."

"Sorry, what?" Chloe asks, a confused look on her face.

"Yeah, what?" I say in a shocked voice too.

My grandma sighs and I can tell she feels bad saying this. "I was given strict orders as to your curfew."

"But, Grandma," I say in disbelief. This was, of course, the lovely work of my parents. "I'm on vacation, remember?"

"But, Alyson, your parents..."

"There is someone here!" I say between clenched teeth, desperately trying to get my grandma not to blow my cover.

"Um...we could just go to the dock," Chloe suggests. "I mean, I kind of just wanted to talk to you and get to know you. It isn't every day that another girl my age ends up staying next door."

I nod.

"I mean if Alyson is allowed to be in the backyard..."

I bury my face in my hands, completely embarrassed.

"The dock is perfectly fine." My grandma smiles.

"Well, follow me..." I say, walking to the dock.

The sun is just preparing to set when we sit down. Chloe lies out on her stomach and I dangle my feet off the side of the dock into the clear water.

"So you have a curfew of nine?" Chloe asks looking at me.

I quickly try to think of something to say that doesn't indicate I'm grounded. "Not exactly," I lie. "My parents and I made a bet about curfews. I told my dad I wouldn't be out past nine every night for a month, if he bought me a new laptop. He agreed but doesn't think I can do it. If I win, I get the computer. If I stay up late, I have to buy him something. He wants me to get more sleep and not stay up too late. I know it doesn't make much sense, but it is just a game my dad and I came up with. My grandma was reminding me." There, I think. That isn't a complete lie.

"Fun!" Chloe says, looking at the sun. "That's a weird way to spend your vacation though."

"I know, but it won't last for much longer. The month is almost up," I say, reminding myself to talk to my grandparents about it.

"That's good."

We are silent for several minutes before Chloe speaks.

"So how is LA?"

"Good," I reply, not really wanting to talk about it. "It is very different than here..."

"I bet! I have always wanted to go, but I end up spending a lot of my vacation time here."

"Yeah, you said you were from Minneapolis, right?"

She nods. "Yep, that's actually where a lot of us kids come from. Our grandparents all live here, so most of us just come up to visit during breaks. We have been doing it for so long now that we all know each other super well."

"Do many other kids come up?"

"Yeah, quite a few actually, but there are only four other kids our age, and they are all guys."

"Let me guess," I say, "is one Marc Maylore?"

"Yeah, he's one of my good friends." She smiles. "Have you met him?"

I nod and tell her what happened earlier in the day.

"That doesn't sound like Marc to me." She pauses. "Wait, you said there were other people with him?"

"Yeah, two."

She smiles. "Okay, so let me guess, one of the other guys had sandy blond hair and a nice tan?"

I laugh. "A nice tan?"

She nods.

"Yeah, I guess. He did have blond hair," I reply.

"That was Eric then. Eric Callaway. He and Marc are super close. He is really fun to be around. Did the other guy have dark brown hair or bleached blond hair?"

"Dark, I think."

She smiles. "That was probably Chris. He lives here year-round, but he doesn't have the greatest influence over Marc and Eric. Somehow, whenever they hang out with him, they end up acting really stupid. They claim they don't like him, which I think is true, but Chris knows everyone, and last I checked, I'm pretty sure Marc and Eric were trying to meet new people and get invited to some of the summer parties and activities. Chris was supposed to be helping with that."

"Oh," I quietly say, looking at the sun's reflection in the calm water.

"I know Marc's first impression may seem bleak, but he is super nice once you get to know him."

I nod and watch the sun drop behind the horizon of little homes across the lake. One moment the ball of fiery orange and red is there, and the next it is gone, leaving the lake a swirl of radiant colors.

The next day I'm woken up at seven. I have breakfast and spend the morning on the phone with one of my friends as she fills me in on life in California. Then I help my grandma make pies for the barbeque, and I assist my grandpa with locating chairs in the garage.

"So why do we need to bring chairs again?" I ask.

"Well, there are a lot of people coming and we will need places to sit, so I said I would bring as many chairs as I could."

"That makes sense," I say, carrying a folding chair to the pile.

The four-car garage itself isn't really used as a garage. Two of the bays store boat trailers for the winter, and the other two hold an old red truck and various items, like the chairs we are gathering.

"Whose place is the barbeque at?" I ask.

"Oh, it is at the Maylores' down the street. They are great people." He smiles.

"So I've heard." I sigh, realizing I will have to see Marc again. "Hey, what is that truck used for?"

"Oh, that old thing?" My grandpa looks up from a cabinet. "I don't use it anymore, but it was the first car I bought after I moved out here from New York. It was a great vehicle."

"Does it still work?" I ask, admiring its shiny red paint.

"Yep. Still runs like new."

"Cool."

"Well, I think we have enough chairs now," he says.

"Is there anything else I can do?" So far my plan of acting pleasant and enjoyable is working well.

He smiles and shakes his head. "Not for me, but you can go see if your grandma needs anything."

I walk out of the garage and across the perfectly green lawn, my bare feet touching the cool grass. Then I run up the wooden porch steps into the kitchen.

"Hi Grandma!" I call as she lines her pies up on the counter.

"Hello, Alyson. Do you mind doing me a favor?"

"Not at all, what do you need?"

"In thirty minutes do you mind running these pies down to the Maylores'?"

I just look at her.

"You don't have to see Marc, just take them to his grandma. Besides, you cannot avoid him forever. We are going to his house. I don't get what happened between you two."

"Fine," I say. "Not a problem." I go upstairs to get ready.

In my room I put on some denim shorts and a white and blue striped shirt. I then do my makeup and curl my hair. I decide that I should try to look my best when meeting most of the neighborhood tonight.

I also decide to be on my best behavior. That way my grandparents will see how I have changed. That is one step closer to getting home.

I go downstairs to collect the pies. My grandma puts them in the bag and writes the address on a piece of paper. "They live at the end of the street, so you can walk."

"Okay," I say, taking the pies.

The walk down the dirt road under the canopy of trees is nice. To my right I see various homes lined up on the shore, and to my left I see the thick forest.

I pass Mr. Bennett's small home and continue down the road. Finally, I reach the end of the street. The last house is a large stone and stucco home. It is two stories and sprawls around the property, by far the largest and prettiest house on the lake.

I stop in the driveway and check the address on the paper my grandma gave me. It's the right house. I don't see anyone in the front yard, so I walk to the front double doors. Halfway there though, I hear a noise. I stop. A faint sound of music seeps into the front from the backyard. I consider ringing the doorbell, but then I decide to walk around back and give the pies to the person back there.

I walk along the side of the gorgeous home and notice one of the large side windows open and I quickly peer in. I see a magnificent stone fireplace that rolls all the way up the inside wall of the house. A large family portrait is hung from it. The living room has fancy leather chairs and art that creates the feel of a rustic-Victorian era. The home reminds me of my own in LA.

The music gets louder, and I now recognize it to be an acoustic guitar. I continue around back until I get to the back deck. I stand behind a tall bush and peer through to see who is making the music. In front of me I see the backside of someone who appears to be Marc. He strums the guitar and hums along. I stand there for a minute listening, because he is amazingly good.

Then the music abruptly stops. "I know you're there," Marc says, turning around and looking at the bush.

Unsure what to do, I step out from behind the bush. "Not bad," I say.

"Oh, it's you again..." he says, looking back at the guitar.

"Yep. Good old me..." I say in a sarcastic tone. I pause. "Are your grandparents here?"

He shakes his head. "No, they ran into town to grab some last-minute things. It's just me and my brother. Can I help you with something?"

"Oh..." I say, not really in the mood for conversation with Marc. "My grandma told me to bring down these pies for the barbeque."

"Cool." He puts his guitar down and stands up. He takes the pies from me and takes them over to a nearby table with a red and white checked tablecloth. "Your grandma always makes the best pies."

I nod.

"Sorry about what I did yesterday," he says, looking at the

ground. "It was stupid to just run away."

"Sorry about the way I acted. It wasn't that bad... I was just being a little dramatic."

"So, um, do you want to come in?" he asks.

"No, I really should be getting back."

"Oh okay, cool," he says, putting his hands in his pocket.

Suddenly I see a figure fly out the back door onto the deck. He stops when he sees me. "You must be the Henderbells' granddaughter."

I nod, looking at a guy in his early twenties. He wears swim trunks and no shirt, revealing his tan, stocky body. He carries a key to a boat in his hand. He has the same golden brown hair as Marc, but his is short and sticks up in the front.

"I have something for your grandma," he says. "Let me go grab it." He turns around and runs back into the house.

"Is that your brother?" I ask.

Marc nods. "Yep, that's Scott."

"Oh," I reply, "I guess I won't be leaving yet then."

"Well, feel free to sit down." Marc points to the porch steps where he has previously been playing guitar.

"That was really good..." I say, trying to start a conversation.

"What was?"

"What you were playing on the guitar. Did you write that yourself?"

"I did, but that's nothing."

"I have heard a lot of guitar music in my life and that wasn't nothing."

"Well, thanks." I'm pretty sure he thinks I am lying.

The two of us fall silent until he speaks. "So what is LA like?"

"You've never been?"

He shakes his head. "I have been to California to surf, but not LA. It's too crazy."

"Oh," I say, not knowing how to respond. "It is really nice there."

"Maybe in Beverly Hills it is, but the rest of it..." He falls silent.

"How do you know I live in Beverly Hills?" I ask. "Did my grandma tell you?"

"No," he says, still not looking at me. "I'm pretty good at reading people."

"Really?" I say, wanting to laugh. "Are you a psychic or something?"

"Do I look like a psychic to you?"

"Okay," I say, "if you think you know me so well, then what am I like?"

He pauses, looks out over the lake, and says, "Okay, you are from LA, and I know you live in Beverly Hills because your mom is some famous model or something like that. Not to mention, when I ran into you yesterday you were carrying some sort of expensive bag. I walked past them in a shop window once."

"Wow," I say sarcastically, "you're good."

"My grandma told me that. Now I will actually read you," he says, part jokingly, and pauses before beginning. "You are one of those girls who just wants to be popular and noticed. You have tons of friends, and a lot of wannabe friends, probably because your mom is famous. So you have a hard time figuring out who to trust. Also, you're one of those people who has a new boyfriend like every week or so. You are never looking for a serious relationship. You have a burning need for attention, and if you could have it your way, you would prefer the world revolved around you. Finally, I feel like you don't want to be here, yet you chose to come on vacation. I still need to figure that out."

I raise my eyebrows at him. I'm completely shocked, and if this Marc guy wanted to try to redeem himself for what he did yesterday, he has just failed.

"Oh, and I almost forgot. What I said at first does have some truth to it, *but behind the way you present yourself, you are really just trying to figure out who you are.*"

I just look at him. Normally if someone had said something like this to me, I would storm off, but there is something real, something genuine, about Marc. It is as if he is telling me this stuff not to offend me, but to gain my trust. And the last thing he said really sticks with me: But behind the way you present yourself, you are really just trying to figure out who you are.

"Okay, I will admit this to you and to you only. You are fairly right, almost right, but only about some stuff."

He smiles.

"Now let me try," I say, assuming I have Marc's personality in the bag.

"Knock yourself out." He laughs, obviously assuming I will fail.

"Well, you are the youngest in your family, and you have an older brother who is in college?"

He nods.

"You come out here in the summer with your grandparents, but it isn't far because you live in Minneapolis."

"You are right, but that's all background knowledge."

"Let's see…" I continue. "You have a real knack for music and you know what you play is good, but you are very humble about the way you present it. In fact I bet you don't play for people much."

"Okay, you got that right. Continue."

"In school you like to keep to yourself, not engaging in many ex-tracurricular activities. You have been in a relationship for a while, it is a serious one, and your best friend is Eric."

He looks at me and bursts out laughing.

"What?" I can tell my face is starting to turn red.

"You really thought you could read me?" He laughs.

"Well, you did it to me."

"Yes, but I have heard stories about you. I practically know you and know what you do."

"Or so you think," I say, feeling embarrassed. He may know the general me, but he has no clue what my life is really like. "Well," I say, taking a deep breath, "if I was so wrong tell me about yourself, Marc Maylore."

He turns his body toward me. "Well, I'm seventeen. I'm cur-rently the captain of the varsity basketball team at my school, and I play golf. I'm a student council representative, and I have a 4.0 GPA. I work very hard in school and in sports. I have many friends and am more extroverted than people think, but in a modest way. I play the guitar, but not many people know that. It is more my special secret. My parents are doctors, so I have been brought up to work diligently and persistently. I love it here at Davis Lake. I love to relax. Eric is my best friend here and in school," he pauses, "so you got some of it right."

"Well, I would have never guessed," I quietly reply.

"Sometimes people can be more deceiving than you think." He winks at me.

Then his brother comes out of the house. "Here you go. Sorry it took so long. I had to write it all out. It is a bill for some porch repair I did last week at your grandparents' place. If you could just have them bring me the money..."

"I will make sure it gets done." I smile, taking the piece of paper.

"Thanks," he calls as he runs toward the dock.

I look at Marc. "I should probably be going now."

"Are you coming to the barbeque tonight?"

"Do you think I really have a choice?"

He just looks at me funny.

"Of course I'm going," I say, in a fake excited tone.

"Well, I will see you there then."

I nod and turn to leave. I am almost out of the yard when I stop. "Marc?" I call, turning back around. "You didn't tell me if I was right about something."

"And what's that?"

"Your relationship status."

"Oh," he says. "I've never been in one."

I laugh. "No really. What is your relationship status?"

"Like I said, I have never been in one."

"A guy like you has never been in a relationship. But you're the captain of the varsity basketball team..."

"That doesn't mean I have never been asked out. I just haven't found the right girl yet. I'm waiting for someone I can really trust."

"Oh," I say, turning to go.

"Now you have to answer a question for me."

"Yes?" I ask, my back turned to him.

"You never told me your name."

"I think you know," I reply.

"I want you to tell me," he softly says.

"Alyson. Alyson Butler." Then I continue out of the backyard not even bothering to look back.

CHAPTER 4

Even when I arrive at the barbeque, I continue to wonder how a person I just met could be so open and honest with me. In those five minutes, I learned more about Marc Maylore than most of his friends probably know. I wish it were that easy to talk to people. To trust them. To tell them the truth. Marc seemed genuine, real, truthful. In those five minutes, I felt as if I had known him for years, but I didn't tell him anything genuine, or real, or truthful about myself. I only told him the lies that everyone else knows, and I wish I hadn't. Except it is too late to tell him now. Besides, he probably won't even care.

I walk around the back of Marc's house with my grandparents. People are spread out in groups all over the deck and the surrounding yard, talking and laughing. In the corner I see an older man at the grill, preparing the burgers and hot dogs. A long table is spread out with various picnic foods, including the pies I brought over earlier.

My grandma and grandpa introduce me to several of their friends, and I act as polite as I can. I want to try to find Chloe, but I cannot find a minute to slip away before being introduced to another neighbor.

Finally, after fifteen minutes, Chloe comes to my rescue.

"There you are!" She smiles. "For a minute there we didn't think you were going to show."

"I was held up talking to people," I say. "And what do you mean 'we'?"

"Marc, Eric, and I."

"I've never even met Eric," I say as she grabs my hand and leads me down toward the docks.

At first all I see is the empty dock with the many Jet Skis and boats that the Maylores have, but when I look back on land, I see a rope swing hanging from a nearby tree. I then see Marc and a tall teenager with sandy blond hair who I assume to be Eric. I also recognize him from the encounter Marc and I had yesterday.

"I found her," Chloe says, still leading me toward the group.

"Hey!" Marc says as he swings slowly back and forth on the swing.

I give a slight nod, acknowledging his hello.

Eric stands up from leaning on the tree. "Well, I guess I'm the last person to meet you. I'm Eric Callaway." He smiles, walking toward me.

"Alyson Butler," I reply.

"Do people ever call you Aly?" Eric asks.

"Um... I guess my brother does..."

"Well, do you mind if I call you Aly?"

I pause, thinking. Honestly I don't think anyone has ever called me Aly other than my brother. I am not sure why though. It seems much easier, shorter. "Not at all," I finally say, smiling.

He nods. "Well, Aly, welcome to Davis Lake."

"Thanks," I reply.

I listen to Chloe, Marc, and Eric's conversations until dinner, not bothering to contribute much, mostly because I have nothing to say, and I don't really know them. Finally we head back to the yard to get something to eat. I wait in line and get a burger with a plethora of fruit and salad sides. Then I follow Chloe and the others to the edge of the deck, where we sit on the bottom step.

"Aly," Marc says, leaning in front of Chloe so he can see me, "any plans this week?"

I shake my head. I would like to say that my plan for the week is to figure out how to get home, but instead I tell Marc that I just want to relax.

"Well if you ever get bored you can always come find Eric and me."

"Yeah," Eric smiles, "we are always around."

"And so am I," Chloe adds.

"Thanks," I reply, making sure to sound as nice as possible, "but I think I will just lie in the sun. I finally get some time to myself. Some time away from my family and siblings, and I'm excited to use it."

I really like the people I'm meeting here, but I didn't come on this trip to make friends. I came here as a punishment, and right now my biggest concern is figuring out how to get back to my normal life. Here everything is too laid back, too easy, and it makes me contemplate my life in LA, which is something I don't want to happen.

"Well, suit yourself," Marc says, leaning back onto the step. We all fall silent.

Toward the end of our meal, I notice two other teenagers standing in the food line. "Who are they?" I ask Chloe, who is sitting next to me.

"That's Chris and Andrew," Eric cuts in.

Chloe shoots him a look.

"Hey, I know them better than you do," he replies.

Marc waves them over as they walk away from the tables carrying large plates of food. "Hey guys!"

"Hi," Andrew replies. Chris nods hello. He was the third guy I saw yesterday with Marc and Eric.

"This is Aly," Marc says. "She is spending the summer with the Henderbells."

"Nice to meet you," Andrew says, extending his hand. He has short bleached-blond hair and a large smile.

"Nice to meet you," I reply.

Chris doesn't say anything. He just looks at me through his dark eyes. He then looks over at Marc and plainly says, "Andrew and I are off to my place. There's nothing exciting going on here."

"I think we are going to play this new video game," Andrew pipes in.

Chris shoots him a look.

"Well, I guess we will see you around then," Marc kindly replies. The two of them begin to walk off.

"They think they are so cool," Chloe sighs as they exit the backyard.

After dinner someone turns on old music and couples begin to dance around the yard. Everyone looks as if they are having a great time. I even see my grandparents dancing.

Marc and Eric run off to go Jet Skiing before the sun goes down. They claim the water is perfect. Chloe and I walk back down to the tree and talk about this summer's styles. Like me, Chloe really enjoys fashion. I find myself sitting on the swing and listening to the faint beat of music in the background and the sound of the small waves lapping on the rocky shore, when suddenly the music stops in the middle of the song. Then I hear the chattering voices go silent. I look at Chloe and she looks at me, and then the two of us look back at the yard.

Up the hill I see that the many small groups of people have condensed into one big group. Two figures stand in front of the group, addressing them, though I cannot make out what they are saying.

"Let's go see what's happening," Chloe says, and the two of us run up toward the deck. As we approach, I once again see Chris and Andrew talking to the group of people.

"I don't know why Marc and Eric try so hard to hang out with them. They just want to go to one of his stupid parties." I can tell she isn't very fond of them. "I wonder what they're up to."

We reach the crowd right as some men are running out of the yard following Chris and Andrew. I then see a lady, who is crying, being escorted out of the group by a man who I guess to be her husband. They, too, follow the group who just left.

I see my grandma, and Chloe and I run up to her. "What's going on?" I ask, a confused look on my face.

My grandma looks at me and says, "Our neighbors, the Blaires, their house was just broken into."

The property stolen from the Blaires' includes $1000 in cash, some expensive jewelry, electronics, a piece of artwork, and Mr. Blaire's loaded handgun. The robbers smashed a window and went about their business.

"I don't get it," Chloe tells me, "I would never think something like this would happen here."

The barbeque clears out quickly. Most people leave to check their homes, or they go down the street to the Blaires'. I stay with Chloe and our grandparents to help the Maylores clean up. Marc and Eric still haven't returned from their ride, but no one seems to care.

"Who would carry out a burglary in daylight?" Chloe asks me as we carry the trash bags to the front of the house.

"Doesn't seem like the brightest plan," I reply, "but whoever did it must have known the barbeque would be going on and everyone would be here."

"Are you saying that someone on this street robbed our neighbors?" She looks offended.

"No," I say calmly, "because everyone was here," I pause, "except Andrew and Chris."

"But they didn't leave that long ago. Plus they had food and plans to go to Chris's down the street. We watched them leave. They aren't capable of that, no matter how much they annoy me."

"But how did they know someone's house was robbed?"

"They saw a strange black car leaving the street, so they went to see where it had come from since they didn't recognize it. They saw the broken glass in the window and ran back here."

"How do you know this?" I ask.

"Because my grandma told me."

"Oh." I throw some trash into the garbage can.

"They will catch whoever did this," Chloe says, sounding reassured. "We have a great police force."

"I'm sure they will," I reply.

CHAPTER 5

My grandma wakes me up at seven again. I don't want to get up, but I force myself to. I have breakfast and spend the beginning of the morning reading for my AP English class and taking notes. It helps me take my mind off life and the events from last night. When I get to a good stopping point, I ask my grandma if I can borrow the house phone again to call a friend. She allows me to, and I dial the number for my friend Tiffany.

She instantly picks up. "Hey, Alyson!"

"Hey, Tiff, do you have a minute?"

"Yeah!" she says. "My family decided to go to our home in Malibu this week, so I'm just lying on the beach."

"That sounds so nice…" I say, imagining the soft sand and the hot sun.

"So how's Minnesota?"

I tell her about the house and the nice people and the small town. I leave out the robbery though.

"That doesn't sound so bad," she says, trying to make me feel better.

"I guess, but there is no shopping, no parties…"

She laughs. "I think you will survive, although I really wish you were here."

"Me too."

"Guess what!" Tiffany says.

"What?"

"The new handbag collections came out!"

"Really?" I say. "I've been looking forward to their release for months."

"I ordered three!" she says excitedly.

"Which brands?"

She pauses. "Oh, just the basics." That's her way of trying to not make me feel bad. She doesn't want to tell me they are all really expensive and really nice. They are probably the ones I want too.

"Your mom let you?" I say, moving the conversation along.

"Of course not. She thinks I have too many, but I did borrow her credit card to get them."

"Won't she notice?" I ask.

"No, she buys too much stuff to notice. When you get home, you have to buy some so we can match!"

I laugh dryly. "I'll still be grounded, remember? My parents won't let me near any type of store."

"Oh…" Tiffany says, "well, we will have to find a way for you to get one."

"Of course we will!" I reply, laughing.

"Oh my god, I have to tell you about what happened last week at Jim Reynolds' party!"

"What?" I say.

She starts to tell me, but I stop listening. My attention is drawn to a shadow outside my door.

"Tiffany," I interrupt.

"Yeah?"

"Hang on one second. My grandma is outside my door. I think she wants something," I whisper.

I get up off my bed and walk over to the door.

"Can I help you, Grandma?" I ask, opening the door. Then I jump back, "Oh my god, Marc!" I nearly yell in shock. "What the heck are you doing here?"

He looks just as disoriented as I am. He opens his mouth to say something, but then I put the phone back up to my ear.

"Alyson?" I hear Tiffany's voice saying. "Is everything okay? Who is Marc?"

"Tiffany, I'm going to have to call you back." I hang up before she can protest or say anything else.

_____

"What are you doing outside my door?" I ask, staring at him.

"Um... I'm still not entirely sure," he replies.

"Not sure?" I say, a little too loudly.

"Well, you see, I was coasting my Jet Ski out front of all the houses because sometimes I like to see the houses and how they are all so different, and your grandpa was outside on his dock and flagged me over. He told me I should take you on a Jet Ski ride and give you a tour of the lake."

"But we have our own Jet Ski," I whisper, looking at the ground.

"Hey, I'm only doing what I'm told. You don't have to go, you know, but it is fun and I'm a good driver."

Though we have our own Jet Ski, I know at this stage in my trip I will not be able to take it out alone. Plus, I don't want to upset my grandpa, or even Marc.

I look at Marc standing in the doorway. "I'll go, but only for a short ride."

"Fine by me," he replies. "I'll just be waiting at the dock," and I hear his footsteps walk down the hall and back down the stairs.

I throw on my swimsuit and put my hair up in a messy bun. Then I grab sunglasses, a life vest, and a towel.

"Where are you going?" my grandma asks.

"Jet Skiing with Marc," I reply as I run out the door.

I greet my grandpa when I get to the dock, and he holds the Jet Ski up to the waterfront while Marc and I climb on.

"You two have fun," my grandpa calls as we coast away from the dock.

The engine of the red Jet Ski sputters as we glide through the perfectly calm water. I look down to see various rocks and clamshells on the sandy lake bottom.

"It's too shallow to start the engine full blast here, but once we get up there," he points ahead, "we will be able to take off."

We continue up some ways before Marc calls, "You ready?"

"Um, where do I hold on?"

"It's me or nothing..."

"Seriously? I hardly know you."

"Suit yourself," Marc says as he brings the engine to life. Instantly the Jet Ski goes roaring across the water, and I have no choice but to wrap my hands around Marc's life vest and hold on for dear life.

I'm pretty sure he makes the engine go full speed, either because he is trying to impress me or because this is what he normally does, which I assume is the more plausible explanation. Nevertheless, it feels amazing to feel the wind and the occasional mist of the water on my face. We glide smoothly across the water as if we are flying, and I can't help but squeal with excitement.

Once at a constant speed, I relax and loosen my grip. Marc takes me around the perimeter of the lake and I get to see all the different houses and boats that dot the shoreline. The lake is quiet, except for several fishing boats, and Marc steers clear of them.

We pass the town docks, and I see the place where I first met Marc. In that moment I never once thought I would talk to him again, let alone have him convince me to go Jet Skiing with him.

I lean my head back and allow the hot sun and the cool wind to splash my face. It is a feeling I have never experienced before, and it is one that brings me comfort. In those several minutes my mind is focused on the now. Not the future or the past. Not this trip and why I am here. I am only focused on the present. The now. And I allow the now to consume my thoughts. For the first time in a while, I allow myself to not think or worry about anything.

I close my eyes and enjoy the ride until I hear the engine slow and then stop. "Are we back already?" I ask, opening my eyes.

"Nope," Marc replies, and as I look around I see we have stopped right in the middle of the lake.

"What are we doing?" I quietly ask.

"Well, since we are out here," he says as he stands up, causing the Jet Ski to shake back and forth uneasily, "I'm going to let you experience something." He turns and sits back down, this time facing directly across from me.

"What do I get the pleasure of experiencing?" I ask, laughing.

"Now, you have been in the water at your grandparents' house, right?"

I nod. "Yeah, I went for a swim in the lake. Why?"

"Good," he replies. "Now give me your hand."

Reluctantly, I give him my hand. He gently touches it and slowly brings it down to the water. He guides my hand into the sparkly dark lake as we lean down.

"Wow!" I say. "It's so much cooler out here."

I look up into his deep blue eyes and he smiles. Then I look back at my hand in the water.

"This cold water has always been my favorite," he explains. "There is something about the way it sends chills through your body. It isn't necessarily cold; it is just natural, real. For some reason, this part of the lake doesn't warm up like the rest does. I have never quite understood it. It's one the deepest parts. It's different from the rest. I just can't explain it."

I pull my hand out of the water and rest it on my knee, allowing the water to drip down my leg. "It's nice," I finally say. "Was that my experience?"

"Only part of it," Marc says.

I'm about to question, but suddenly Marc stands up and jumps into the water. The Jet Ski rocks back and forth and I grab onto the side for support.

Marc surfaces and grabs the side of the watercraft. He runs his hand through his golden brown hair and pushes it back.

"What are you doing?" I ask.

"Well, you have to feel the best water in the lake. It truly is amazing," Marc gushes in a sarcastic voice. "Come on!" He laughs, splashing water up onto my leg.

I shudder as the cool water hits my leg. "Hey!" I yelp, pulling my leg back. I lean down and splash him with water in the face, but he grabs my hand and pulls me down. I lose my balance and tumble into the deep blue water.

I come up discombobulated and gasping for air. I reach for the side of the Jet Ski and place my sunglasses, which I rescued on the way in, up on the seat. Then I push my hair out of my eyes. "Marc! Not fair!"

"Hey, I had to get you in somehow," he calmly says.

For the next several minutes, the two of us float on our backs with our feet on the edge of the Jet Ski in serenity. The water really is colder here, but not in an uncomfortable way. It is refreshing, as Marc described.

"All right," Marc says, disturbing the peace, "time to go."

He twists his body around and grabs onto the Jet Ski. I do the same. "Hey, Marc," I smile, "can I drive it back?"

"Are you fully licensed?"

"What do you think?" I say in an offended voice, though I'm only playing. "I'm seventeen."

"Okay," he replies, "but you're supposed to be eighteen to operate it."

"Really?"

"Yeah, but we all do it anyways. No one ever checks." He smiles. "Now let's see if you can drive this thing as fast as I can!" Marc laughs as I turn the engine on.

Then I straight shot it full speed back to my dock.

———○———

My grandpa has gone in when we get back, and I figure the ride has been about thirty minutes. Marc lines the Jet Ski up with the dock and grabs the side so I can step right off onto it. "Thanks for the ride," I say, taking off my life jacket and throwing it on the plastic surface.

"Thanks for going," he replies.

We fall silent. "Do you want to come in or something?" I ask, pointing to the house.

"Thank you for the offer, but I have to get back to my house."

"Oh, okay, no problem."

"Sorry," he says.

"Well, see you later."

"Yep, see you!" he calls as he begins to coast the Jet Ski away from the dock.

Once Marc is not looking back at me, I turn around and run up the hill and into the house.

"How was it?" my grandpa asks me when I enter through the screen door.

"Good," I say, walking across the living room.

"Do you need something?" my grandpa asks.

"Where is the phone?"

"Ah, wanting to finish up your call from earlier." He smiles.

"Yes..."

"It's upstairs on the bed in my bedroom."

"Thanks!" I run toward the stairs.

I grab the phone from the room and then enter mine. I slip a white cover-up over my damp swimsuit.

I do not call Tiffany back though. Instead, I dial a different number. The phone rings, and rings, and rings, and I'm brought to voicemail. "Hi, this is Matthew, can't get to the phone right now, but I'll try to call you back!" Then I get a beep to leave a message.

I hang up. "Dang it," I whisper. I look at the phone. There is one more number I can try. I sigh and dial. It begins to ring. *Please pick up. Please pick up.*

"Hello, this is the Butlers' house," I hear a little girl say into the receiver.

"Lily, is that you?"

"Yes," the young voice replies.

"Thank god," I whisper. "Lily, this is Alyson."

"Hi Alyson," Lily says. "How's your trip?"

"Fine," I say quickly.

"Do you want to talk to Mommy?"

I cringe, just what I was dreading. "No! No, Lily, I need you to take the phone to Matthew."

"Why don't you want to talk to Mommy?"

I take a deep breath. "Because I need to talk to Matthew."

I hear movement on the other end of the line.

"Lily, whatever you do, do NOT take the phone to Mommy!" I yell urgently into the phone, but I get no reply, only the background noise of movement. Then I hear breathing on the other line. Someone else has just received the phone.

"Hello?" I hear a voice say.

"Oh my god, Matt, you actually got the phone," I say with relief.

"Aly, is everything okay?"

"Yeah, it's fine now," I say, calming myself down. I thought Lily was going to take the phone to Mom."

"Hey, for a seven-year-old she takes pretty damn good instructions. Anyway, is everything okay over there?"

"Matt, language," I say.

"Yeah, yeah. Speak for yourself. Is it bad?" he asks.

"I wish. I wish I could say it sucked, but the more time I spend here, the nicer the people are and the more fun I have." I pause. "I can't believe I just admitted that."

"Isn't that a good thing?"

"I guess, but I was hoping it would suck so I could come home."

"Aly, I get that you want to come home..."

"Yes. No. Not really. I don't know. Actually, when I think about it, I realize that the people here actually care about me. I don't necessarily want to come home. I just want to come home to prove to Mom and Dad that they were wrong."

"Aly, you have to let that go..."

"Matt, I didn't call you to lecture me on life," I snap.

"Sorry," he says. "Well, what do you need?"

"I need you to do me a favor."

"Shoot."

"I need you to go into my closet."

"Okay," he says. "One sec, I'm walking down the hall, now I'm turning the corner." Then he stops talking and I hear him yelling something.

"Sorry, Mom wanted to know who I was talking to."

"What did you say?"

"I said I was talking to a friend."

"Thanks," I reply. "I'm surprised she's home and wondering for once."

He doesn't reply to that. "Okay, I'm in your closet; what do you need?"

"I need you to grab a duffle bag from one of my shelves and fill it with any clothing that isn't silky, sparkly, or super expensive. I am way overdressed for this trip. I need you to find all the casual clothes you can find: shorts, tank tops, and T-shirts. Then ship them out here for me."

I can tell he has put the phone on speaker, and I can hear him walking back and forth opening drawers and shuffling through hangers.

"Dang, Aly, why can't you have a normal-sized closet? I swear your closet is bigger than most people's master bedrooms."

"I like clothes."

"Obviously," he replies. "Aly, if you are going to try to come home so bad, why do you need these clothes?"

"I don't think I am going to come home early. I mean not now."

"Really?" he says, sounding skeptical.

"I just don't have the reason I need to come home." I say. "I have been trying so hard to find a reason. I have been trying to be sent home, but I just can't."

"Oh," he says. "Well, I will make sure you have the clothes."

"Only twenty-seven more days," I tell him.

"Hey, you will be home in time for my sixteen and two-month birthday."

"Yep. I wouldn't want to miss my brother's sixteen and two-month birthday," I say sarcastically.

He laughs.

"Hey, I should probably go. I don't know how long I can talk to 'a friend' on the home phone."

"Well, next time make sure you have your cell phone on."

"I actually left it at the beach yesterday."

"What were you doing at the beach?" I ask.

"Tanning. It was the middle of the day too. What do you think I would be doing?"

"I don't know," I reply.

"Anyway, Dad said he would buy me a new one this afternoon."

"Dad would never do that for me," I mutter. "Hey, speaking of phones, is there any chance you could throw mine in the box?"

"Sorry, sis, no can do," Matt tells me. "I can send you clothes, but that is it. I'll make sure you have them in two days."

"Okay, thanks, Matt."

"No problem," he kindly replies.

"Oh, and Matt!" I yell right as he is about to hang up.

"Yeah?"

"Please don't do anything stupid this summer."

"Don't worry, Aly. I won't. I'm not like you. Besides, I'm aware of the consequences."

"Okay, bye, Matt."

"Bye, Aly."

I hang up and slide down the empty bedroom wall I'm standing against. How is it possible that I suddenly had a change of heart? For the last three days, I have been wanting to get home, and now I want to throw it all away. Why? I ask myself and I suddenly know. It was the Jet Ski. The water. The conversation. The feeling of being trusted. It was Marc.

CHAPTER 6

In the evening, Chloe and her grandparents decide to join us for a dinner of spaghetti and meatballs. We eat. We laugh. And I get to know a lot more about the lake itself and Chloe.

Though I never expected it, Chloe is beginning to open herself up to me, and I have slowly done the same for her, kind of. We have a lot in common, a passion for traveling, fashion, life outlooks. Although I am pretty sure Chloe has never gotten herself into some of the stuff I have.

Chloe and her grandparents leave after sunset, which is nine o'clock. I guess it is late, but not for me. I help my grandma with the dishes, and when they are done, the three of us find ourselves on the porch all alone.

We talk, and I tell them about Matt, Lily, and my other brother, Jake, who is ten. As the sky changes from a fiery orange and red to a pale purple, my grandpa says, "How about I make you two my famous drink."

"And what is that?" I ask.

"It is secret," he replies. "But I do need to run into town and buy some cans of soda. The stores here always stay open late in the summer."

"I will go!" I offer as he begins to stand up. My grandparents have already lightened up on the curfew rule.

"That would be just fine." He smiles, and I run into the house. Upstairs, in my room, I open up my wallet to grab my driver's license. I reach into the small slot it is usually in, but I don't feel it. I suddenly panic. Where could it be? I never drive anywhere without it and I haven't used it since I got here.

I run back downstairs onto the porch. Both my grandma and my grandpa turn to look at me.

"Have you seen my license?" I ask, but then a thought reaches me.

They both look at me.

"You took it. Didn't you?"

"Well, you see…" my grandma begins, but I cut her off.

"No. My parents told you to take it. So I wouldn't go anywhere. They know I won't drive without it. It was them…"

"Sweetie, we forgot about that. You see, there were certain rules that your parents gave us when you arrived, like no electronics, no driver's license." She tries to name more, but I cut her off again.

"Even here they really don't trust me," I whisper, tears beginning to well in my eyes. And then I turn and run out the front door.

I slam the screened door behind me and run toward the garage. I hear my grandma calling after me, but I don't turn around. I can't talk to anyone right now. Besides, I don't want to hurt my grandparents, and I fear if I stick around, that is exactly what will happen. I am better off left alone.

In the garage I scan the objects. I see the red truck, then some boating equipment, and finally a bike, just what I was looking for. Quickly I half drag, half wheel the bike out the door. I scramble on, and pedal out of the drive.

On the road I pedal hard and fast. I look straight ahead. I let my frustrations boil inside me, emotions about my parents, their stupid excuses, and refusal to trust me. They only know half the story, and even the part they know isn't all true. They don't want to hear my reasons for doing what I did. In their minds, it is entirely my fault, and they did nothing wrong.

It's only when I got here that they started caring, only here that they suddenly wanted to monitor my behavior and actually make rules. But that pisses me off because they aren't even here. They haven't been here in years. They haven't cared about this place until they realized they could get rid of me here. They don't

---

even know what it's like here, yet they are determined to show my grandparents they are good parents and try to dictate every aspect of my life. They took my license, but they have no clue that there is nowhere for me to drive to except the stupid grocery store.

I'm grounded, and I understand that, but if my parents really want me to learn a lesson, they would have my grandma and grandpa make the rules, because they actually care.

By now I'm on the two-lane highway. On both sides of me I see rolling fields of fresh green corn and luscious big oak trees. The crickets sing their songs, and the birds chirp their good nights as they prepare for bed.

I breathe hard, panting. The wet, humid air clings to my clothes and skin, making it feel sticky. My legs burn as I pedal, but I don't stop. I can't stop. The burn takes my mind off the thoughts, and I know the moment I stop, they will all come rushing back.

It's nearly dark now, and I know I will lose all light in a matter of minutes. I ride my bike across the empty road to the other side where I begin to pedal back. I don't see a single car in the time I'm out there, but that is only because it is late. My guess is that it's nearly ten.

I'm almost back to my street when I see my first car of the night. I see its bright headlights ahead, but this car approaches me quickly. It's when the car nearly runs me off the road that I realize it's driving way over the speed limit. It swerves into the other lane at the last second, and I rapidly veer my bike off the road, falling into the ditch on the roadway. I stand up quickly to see the speeding vehicle turning onto my street. I squint to make out the car and I instantly recognize it as a black Range Rover.

I brush myself off, and get my bike back on the road. Luckily I'm not injured, though I do have a scrape on my leg from sliding down the gravelly ditch. A small amount of blood begins to ooze from the cut, but it doesn't bother me.

My adrenaline is pumping, and I can feel my heartbeat pounding against my chest. *I was almost hit by a car. I was almost hit by a car.* That thought keeps running through my mind as I bike back up the road.

Finally, I reach the road that leads to the house. It splits off in two directions, to the right, which will take me home, and to the left. I do not turn to the right though. Instead I turn the other way, deciding to make a quick stop.

My tires roll under the dark canopy of trees that sway their dancing branches above me. I can hear the waves gently hitting the shore and the gravel crunching beneath my weight. I pass Mr. Bennett's house, and finally I come to the end of the road and stop my bike in front of the last house, the Maylores'.

Most of the home's lights are turned off, except two upstairs, which I assume to be Marc's and Scott's. I look in the driveway to see a black Range Rover. I recognize it as the one parked outside Mr. Bennett's and assume it must be Marc's. I begin to approach it to see if its engine is warm when I hear the front door open.

I stop and look up toward the door. A figure, which I make out to be Marc, shines a flashlight in my face. "Aly? What are you doing here?" he quietly asks.

Hands covering my face, and blinded by the light, I hiss, "What the heck were you doing driving like some lunatic tonight?"

"What?" I can't see his face, but I know he knows.

"The Range Rover is yours, right?"

"Yeah..."

"And you were driving tonight. Right?"

"I was..."

"Then what's wrong with you?" I say, raising my voice.

"Shhhh, be quiet," he whispers.

"You almost ran me over! I will not stop yelling! What were you doing, like ninety in a thirty-five?"

By now he has come down the stairs and has shined the light away from me and onto the concrete driveway. He simply looks at me. "Get in the car."

"What?" I say, shocked by his response.

"Get in the car," he plainly says, unlocking the doors and walking toward the driver's seat.

"Marc, I don't think you understand, I'm not getting in that car."

"Just please get in and I can explain," he says, hopping in his seat and opening the passenger door.

"No, I'm not getting in a car with a stranger..."

"Aly, I am not a stranger."

"I have only known you for...four days."

"Please get in. I'm not going to do anything crazy," he coaxes.

"No," I say, crossing my arms like a child.

He takes a deep breath. "Please, Aly, please trust me."

Those words send a shiver up my spine. Those are the words I have been itching to hear. Those words I desperately need to hear. I take a deep breath and consider my options.

"Fine." I slide into the passenger seat.

⟫⟪◑⟫⟪

The car's luxurious interior reminds me of home and helps me calm myself. I sit rigid and still though, deliberately not making eye contact with Marc. He cautiously backs out of the driveway, and I wonder how the suddenly hesitant driver could have been so reckless earlier. He turns his headlights on and slowly begins to idle down the road.

When he turns up onto the main road, I know something is up. I guess I thought he could have been taking me home, but I should have known better. Why would he drive me six houses down the way?

"Okay, Marc, what are we doing?" I ask, annoyed, finally breaking the silence.

"Well," he begins, "this is kind of a personal question, but how are your grades?"

I roll my eyes. "What do grades have to do with this?" I ask, beginning to regret getting in the car.

"Okay, what I mean is, do you ever get stressed in school?"

"Like you, I have a 4.0, and yes I do."

"You got a 4.0 junior year of high school?" he says, a hint of surprise in his voice.

"Yeah, I did actually. I worked harder than you would think."

"Oh." He laughs. "I thought you would have been more likely to go out and party than study."

"You have no idea..." I say, quietly looking away. "Anyway, what do school and stress have to do with all this?"

"Well, when you get stressed, what do you do?" he asks, turning onto the two-lane highway and driving the speed limit.

"I leave."

"Leave?" He looks at me, confused.

"I leave my house. I just can't concentrate there, so I go somewhere else."

"Where?"

"Wow, you want specifics tonight," I dryly say.

"Sorry," he says, awkwardly shifting positions in his seat and keeping his eyes on the road.

I don't respond.

"Anyway," he continues, "I know this is going to sound bad, and I know it is bad, but..."

"You go out at night when no cars are around and drive the road with crazy fast speeds because it lowers your stress levels, and you do it here because it has become some sort of addiction," I finish.

He just looks at me.

"What? Did you forget you almost ran me over like a half hour ago?"

"Well, I guess that sums this conversation up," he says, keeping his hands tightly gripped on the wheel.

"So, you brought me all the way out here in your car to tell me you have extreme driving problems?"

"Well, yes, but I also took you out here to show you."

"Show me?" I raise my voice unintentionally. "No way. You almost..." But I don't finish my sentence before he steps on the gas.

The car goes rolling by the endless cornfields faster and faster every second. I look over to the speedometer to see the speed climbing from thirty, to forty, to fifty.

He rolls down all the windows and turns the radio on so that the noise can be heard even with all the wind blowing through the car. I instantly recognize the song as Lana Del Rey's "Ride."

"Hold on!" he yells over the noise. I grasp the bar above my head and hold on for dear life as we reach ninety.

We zoom down the perfectly straight, never-ending highway, wind blowing in my hair and music blasting. "Relax!" Marc calls to me. "I do this all the time, remember?"

I shake my head, refusing to relax, but over time I loosen up and release the handgrip. "Do you know the song?" I ask.

He nods.

"Me too!" I yell back.

"Singalong!" he suggests, turning his head from the road to look at me.

"No way! And keep your eyes on the road!"

He looks back. "Come on!" He smiles. "I'll do it with you."

I laugh trying to picture the guy next to me singing.

"Ready?" Marc yells over the noise. "One, two, three!"

I force my mouth open and we sing together.

I burst into laughter. "That's the best you can sing?"

"It's my best car singing!"

I throw my head back in my seat and let my arm hang out the car window. The crisp night air feels amazing as it rushes in and out of the car, blowing my hair around. He laughs too, and between our laughing and gasps for air, the two of us manage to yell and sing the rest of the song out the window of the speeding car.

When the song ends, we gradually slow back down to the normal speed limit again. Marc rolls up the windows and turns down the radio so it softly plays in the background.

"In the time I drive like that, my mind clears and I forget about everything going on in my life. Sometimes I feel I put too much pressure on myself. I feel like I live on a level of stress, and I feel that failure isn't an option. I just have so much I can't mess up...and my parents have certain expectations of me. I have tried countless things to try to hide my worries, but this thing, though completely reckless and illegal, seems to work the best. I like the adrenaline. I'm so sorry that I almost ran you off the road earlier. I need to be more careful. I just was in my own world. My world, where everything is okay." He pauses as we turn back onto the main road. "I can't believe I'm telling this to a stranger." He suddenly stops, embarrassed, and looks away from me, keeping his eyes dead set on the road.

"I'm not a stranger, remember? I think we all do pretty stupid things when we can't think straight, and all we look for are people we can trust, people who can understand what we are going through."

"I have never told anyone what I do, besides Eric, because I know there would be consequences. It's just that when I scared you on the road, I felt I needed to show you that I didn't want to hurt you. I was just doing what I do. Besides, I wouldn't have hit you. I have mastered the instant swerve..."

"Don't worry, your secret is safe with me, but honestly, Marc, I think you need to be careful. You probably don't want to hear this from me, but you could get yourself in some serious trouble if you keep this up," I say, trying to sound stern but kind.

"I know...and I'm trying. It's just that everyone expects so much from me and I can't be perfect."

I can tell Marc is slowly starting to break down, and though I still barely know him, I feel bad for him. Obviously, there is a lot more going on under the surface of the guy with the perfect life. "Marc, just stop for tonight. You look really tired, and I think you are starting to work yourself up."

"You know what? You're right," he says, sighing. "I'm so sorry for making you listen to my problems."

We pull up in front of my house. We sit quietly in the car for another minute before I step out onto the driveway, closing the door behind me.

"I'll drop the bike off tomorrow," Marc tells me.

"Okay, thanks."

"I really am sorry."

"Hey, we all need people to talk to once in a while." I smile at him. "Thanks for the ride."

"No, thank you," he replies.

CHAPTER 7

My grandma and grandpa are worried sick when I arrive home, but I'm not punished for running off, which is a change. They just accept the fact that I needed to get away and that this is a hard time in my life. They ask me what happened to my leg and I simply reply that I had fallen while riding my bike, which is partially true. They are also extremely happy when I say Marc found me and gave me a ride home.

"So, Alyson," my grandma asks me the next morning while making lunch, "what are you going to do today?"

"Relax, sit, I don't know," I reply, grabbing the lunchmeat from the fridge.

"You should go hang out with your friends," my grandpa chimes in.

"They're not my friends yet, Grandpa," I say. "I only just met them."

"Well, you seem to be spending an awful lot of time with them for saying they are strangers, especially Chloe and Marc."

I sigh and pull my long hair into a messy bun. "I don't go to them, they come to me."

"Well, they probably want to get to know you better," my grandpa says. "It isn't every day another teenager shows up in this small town. Maybe you should open up to them."

I look at him, unsure how to respond.

"You miss your friends in LA, don't you?" my grandma asks.

"You have no idea," I reply as I open the bread bag for sandwiches.

"Well, use this opportunity to make new friends. You are here for several more weeks. Make the best of it. You won't regret meeting someone new."

The room falls silent as we make sandwiches. My grandma leaves to go change the laundry.

"Grandpa, did my mom like it up here?"

He smiles. "She loved it. Had lots of friends. There were always events going on, family time..."

I'm about to ask what happened and why she stopped coming, but my grandma comes back.

"Alyson, there is someone at the door who wants to talk to you."

"Oh, okay," I casually say, leaving the kitchen and walking to the front door. The rest of the conversation will have to wait.

When I come around the corner and look out the screen door, I see a somewhat familiar face.

"Eric?" I say, completely confused as to why this guy is at my door.

"Hey, Aly," he awkwardly says, forcing an unnatural smile.

"Can I help you?" I ask, opening the door. "Chloe and Marc aren't here."

"Oh, I know," he replies, "I actually came to ask you something."

"Okay," I say waiting for him to speak.

"Well, first of all I brought your bike back from Marc's and set it up against the garage."

"Thank you," I say.

"And also, Marc and I were wondering if you wanted to go tubing with us. You see, normally we go with Scott or Chloe, but Scott is helping some neighbors and Chloe went to town for the day. We need a third person for the spotter, and so we were just wondering if you were interested."

"Um...." I reply, not quite sure how to respond. I look back into the house to see if my grandparents are nearby. I see my grandpa in the kitchen, and he must have heard the conversation because he waves his hand coaxing me to go.

"Sure... I will spot for you guys," I say in an uneasy voice.

"Sweet!" Eric says with a look of relief. "Let's go! I have my car right here so we can just drive down to Marc's."

I look at an old red jeep parked in the driveway. "Do I need anything?" I ask.

He shakes his head. "Just a swimsuit, but it looks like you already have that."

I look down at the blue straps of my bikini showing from my cover-up. "Okay," I say, stepping down the stairs.

I have never actually been tubing before, so I don't quite know what to expect. Fortunately, the lake is calm, so I don't have to worry about waves and bumps that could possibly throw me into the water.

Eric drives me down the street, and we pull into Marc's driveway. I prepare to open my door, but Eric stops me. "Hey," he says, "before you go, you might want this." He hands me a pink long-sleeved shirt with big letters of a surf shop written across it. "What's this?" I ask, taking the shirt.

"Swim shirt...you'll need it too, especially when we hit the bumps." He grins at me.

"Whose is it?" I ask, fingering the obviously worn shirt.

"Chloe's." He opens the car door and gets out. I do the same.

"Will she mind?" I ask as Eric begins to jog around the side of the house.

"Nope, she left it in my car a couple weeks ago when we floated down the creek, and hasn't bothered to get it out," he calls back to me. "Now come on!"

———◦《◦》◦———

Down at the dock, Marc has already hooked the yellow and red tube to the Jet Ski, which sits on the dock waiting to be used. He loads something into one of the compartments of the Jet Ski and sits back on the seat when he sees us coming.

"I see you decided to join us!" Marc calls to me, smiling and waving.

"I did," I reply, stepping onto the dock.

"We're all set to go." He steps off the Jet Ski and onto the hard plastic dock. He puts on a blue swim shirt, like the one I have, but for guys, and then buckles up a life vest.

"Hey, Butler," Eric says to me as he does the same, "you'll need this." He tosses me a purple and black life jacket, and I put it on after slipping on Chloe's shirt. I quickly braid my hair to prevent it from getting tangled in the wind.

"Okay," Marc says. "Eric, you will go first, I will drive, and Aly can spot."

"That way I can show you all how it's done!" Eric grins.

"Spot?" I ask.

"Yeah, you sit on the back of the Jet Ski and watch to make sure Eric is okay and doesn't fall in." He then quickly shows me the hand signals that Eric could use while riding. They are simple, like a thumbs-up for faster, so I don't think I will have a problem.

Marc lowers the water machine off the lift into the lake. The two of us climb on, and he starts the engine so it begins to idle out into the water.

I unravel the towrope, while Eric hops on the tube as it is pulled out behind us. "All the slack is out," I tell Marc, and he replies, telling me to make sure Eric is ready.

Eric gives me a thumbs-up, and I tell Marc we are ready to go. Marc looks back at Eric though before going. "You better hang on, sucker!" he calls to him, laughing.

"Bring it on!" Eric calls back. I get the feeling the two of them do this a lot and know how to push each other's buttons while tubing. Marc has seemed to return to his old friendly and funny self after his near breakdown last night. In fact, I'm pretty sure he is pretending it didn't even happen, which is fine with me.

The engine roars to life, pulling Eric up out of the water. Marc holds the gas down, making the Jet Ski gain speed, and at some point I swear he is driving faster than one should while pulling a tube. Then again it is Marc, and I guess I have come to kind of accept that he is a reckless driver...no matter what he is driving.

I watch Eric as he holds on to the tube. He lets out a yell of excitement. His face shows pure joy. He reminds me of a little kid, excited about every little thing, and it makes me laugh to myself.

The lake is fairly calm today, and as we zoom across it, Marc drives in circles in order to produce waves from the wake. After several minutes I notice that Eric throws his arms up in the air when he is not concerned with tipping over, and holds on during Marc's crazy driving sessions. I get the impression though that Marc and Eric live for trying to disrupt each other's tubing experiences.

Finally we switch and this time Eric drives while Marc tubes. Eric basically drives the same way, and Marc tries to show off by holding on the least amount of time as possible. His ride looks crazy because he is constantly being swerved from side to side, hitting bumps and abrupt turns. It looks a little too scary for me and I hope that when my turn comes, the two of them will drive more rationally. I keep thinking that Marc will be thrown into the water any second, but he manages to stay on.

When Marc's turn is up, I pull in the rope as Eric brings the Jet Ski to an idle. I pull the tube up against the boat so we can swap positions. "Ready?" Marc asks me, out of breath from his ride, which is weird since all he had to do was hold on.

"Yes, but you two need to swear to drive like sane people."

"What? You don't like our style, Butler?" Eric asks, pretending to look offended.

"Drive normally..." I say to him, glaring.

"Normally is a little vague," Marc replies in a joking tone.

"Well, the moment one of you drives how you just did, I. Will. Kill. You. Are we clear?"

"Don't worry, Aly," Marc reassures me. "You will enjoy your ride."

I hop into the now empty tube as Marc pushes the rope and me out into the water. I give him a thumbs-up when I am ready. Eric drives the tube up and on top of the water. He starts off insanely fast, but then slows to a calm, steady speed, when he remembers what I told him.

I love the feel of the wind blowing and the constant spray of water in my face. I love how I can see the whole shore from where we are, and I can look at the little dots of houses and trees. I love the look of the metallic water as I glide over it and how I can see my reflection when I am forced out of the wake into the calm water. I throw my head back and let my arms hang out, and for once in my life I just enjoy myself.

I sit like that for a couple more minutes before looking back up at Marc. The wind blows his golden brown hair, and at times he has to push his bangs from his eyes. He makes a hand motion of up and down, and it takes me a minute to realize that he means bumps. I shake my head, but he doesn't listen and tells Eric to drive back over the waves produced by our wake. The speed increases and before I know it, I'm screaming my butt off while hitting the small bumps that send my tube flying off the top of the water.

I guess I scream too much because Eric and Marc slow the Jet Ski down back to an idle. "You okay?" Marc calls, looking concerned.

"Yes!" I laugh. "I'm great!"

"Okay, but it's time to switch," he says, pulling me toward the watercraft. "I thought there was actually something wrong with you."

"Nope," I call back to him. "Just being dramatic, as usual."

Suddenly, I feel my tube being lurched toward the Jet Ski. Then the tube abruptly stops again and so does the power of the machine. I'm not all the way reeled in, but I am close enough to hear Eric curse rather loudly.

"What happened?" Marc asks urgently, looking at Eric, who has remained silent this whole time.

"The rope was sucked into the motor…" Eric says, sounding angry. "Shit," he says, desperately, looking at Marc.

"You're kidding, right?"

He shakes his head.

"So we're stuck out here then?" Marc says, trying to stay calm.

"You brought your phone though."

"Eric, I thought you were…"

They look at each other.

Seeing that they are both slightly frazzled, I pull myself in the rest of the way to the Jet Ski, and grab onto the side.

"God, how did we forget a phone again?" Eric asks.

"This has happened before?" I interject.

Marc shakes his head.

"Well, what are we going to do?" I ask.

"We could wait for a boat to pass," Eric glumly suggests.

"Nah, too long..." Marc says, scanning the empty horizon.

The three of us fall silent until Marc speaks again. "I know. There's my house." He points into the distance. "It can't be more than a mile and a half. I can just swim to shore, grab the other Jet Ski, and tow us back."

"You're really going to swim?" Eric asks.

"Yeah, I placed first for the boys free style in junior high. I still swim." Marc begins to take his life jacket off.

"Don't you want to think this through a little more?" Eric asks.

"Nope, I want to get back as soon as possible." He jumps into the water. "I will be right back. You guys wait here!"

Eric tries to protest, but Marc has already begun to swim.

"Well, that went well..." Eric says, turning to face me on the tube.

I climb off the tube and hop up on the bench next to Eric. The tube, being so stuck in the engine, doesn't move at all.

"That was impulsive," I reply. "I hope he'll be okay out there."

"Oh, don't worry. Marc will be fine. Unlike most people, Marc is a man of many talents."

"So I have heard." I stretch my legs out into the water. "Well, Eric, since we're stranded out here with nothing to do, how about you tell me a little about yourself."

"There isn't much to tell. I live in Minneapolis and go to the same school as Marc. I play basketball and spend my summers here. That's about it."

"Hey, keeping it simple is always nice." I smile. "So...you and Marc must have a lot in common."

"I guess." He looks out at the swimming Marc, who is getting farther and farther away from the watercraft and closer and closer to the shore. "I mean, we share the same passion for sports, like basketball and golf. We have done so much together and I consider him to be like a brother, but when I think about it, we're really different. I mean, he is a straight-A student, and he's so dedicated to school. Me, on the other hand...not as much. I have made so many stupid mistakes in my short life, and he seems to always be riding on a clean slate."

"What kind of mistakes?"

"You probably wouldn't understand, just stupid peer pressure stuff that you regret after doing it."

"No, I know what you mean," I quietly reply.

"I mean I'm not a bad kid. I don't want to do anything to ruin my life. I never would do anything like that. I always try to weigh the consequences, at least now. I just don't understand how Marc has always managed to be so perfect. It's as if he has never put himself in a bad situation. I'm making myself sound like some crazy drug addict, aren't I?"

I shake my head. "No. We all make mistakes. I mean choosing to not study for a test can be a stupid peer pressure mistake."

"Yeah, that's exactly what I mean."

"And Marc has had to have made some mistakes in his life."

"Little ones, I guess, but nothing like I have," Eric says, staring out onto the lake. His slight jealousy of Marc begins to seem apparent. "Anyway, enough about me. How are you liking it here?"

"It's nice, and I think I like it more and more every day. It's definitely not what I expected."

"Yeah, small towns can be deceiving." He winks.

I move my toes back and forth in the water, creating little ripples. "Not like that." I quietly laugh. "I just didn't expect to meet so many people my age who are actually remotely fun to be around."

"Yeah, I know I'm pretty cool," Eric jokes. "Chloe is super chill and fun, and I know she's thrilled that there is finally another girl her age up here, and not just us guys. There's only so long we can listen to her talk about fashion."

"Yeah, she's super nice, and Marc is really friendly too."

We fall silent for several minutes. I look out around the lake and stare at the sun's reflection across the ripples.

"I think Marc likes you," Eric finally says.

I look at him. "Likes me?"

He nods. "Ever since he met you, he can't seem to stop indirectly bringing you up in conversations. I've never seen him act this way with a girl before."

"Oh," I say, not quite sure how to respond.

"Don't worry, he's really shy and my guess is he will never tell you." Eric laughs. "Anyway, where is Marc?" We look out into the water.

"Well," I say, making sure the subject has been changed, "he either made it back or he drowned."

Shortly after we stop seeing Marc, he drives up with the other Jet Ski.

"I see he didn't drown," I tell Eric as Marc stops to tie his Jet Ski to the broken one.

"Thanks for the faith in me, guys," Marc says. We just laugh.

"How was your dip in the lake?" Eric asks.

"It was grand, just grand," Marc replies in some weird accent.

———— ◦((◦))◦ ————

I'm deeply relieved when we hit shore again. Though the lake wasn't bad, sitting there wasn't super entertaining. Eric and Marc head up to the garage to try to find tools to pull the rope out of the motor. I decide to go home.

"Eric," Marc says, "go inside and see if Scott is home yet. This is the perfect job for him to help us with."

Eric runs in the house, leaving Marc and me in the front yard.

"Sorry about this tubing experience," Marc says.

"No problem."

"I hope you didn't mind Eric's company."

"No, it was good. We just talked."

"About?"

"School...stuff like that."

"Cool," Marc says, smiling.

I don't look him in the eye directly.

"We will have to go tubing again and actually get more than one run each in," he tells me.

"Yeah." I smile.

"Well, maybe I will see you tomorrow."

"Yeah, tomorrow," I reply. "Bye, Marc."

"Bye, Aly."

It is on my walk back that Eric's words about Marc finally begin to sink in. *"I think Marc really likes you..."*

Surely that cannot be true. He just met me. I just met him. I'm not even that likable of a person.

Eric could be completely wrong or just messing with me, but I think I trust Marc. I also think I trust Eric. I try reasoning with myself only to discover that the more I think about it, the more I decide that staying away from Marc might be the best idea. I didn't come here this summer to fall for a boy or have one fall for me.

CHAPTER 8

My grandparents find the story of Marc, Eric, and me getting stranded in the lake extremely funny. Honestly, they have no sympathy for me; they're too busy laughing about Marc swimming to shore and me and Eric having to wait.

The next day I go into town with my grandma. We go to the small grocery and comb the aisles, looking for common ingredients the store cannot seem to provide. Then we have lunch at the town's bistro. For being in the middle of nowhere, the food here is excellent.

"Thank you for lunch," I tell my grandma as we arrive back at the house midafternoon.

"My pleasure." She beams. "Glad I could spend some quality time talking to you."

"It's always fun," I reply. The more time I spend with my grandma, the more I feel like I have known her forever. She is always there to listen to me, and for once in my life it is nice to have someone around who actually wants to hear what I have to say.

I grab a couple of bags of groceries and follow my grandma up the porch steps and into the house. I set the bags on the counter and begin to unload them when I see something out of the corner of my eye. "Hey, look," I call to my grandma, "my box of clothes from Matthew came!"

"It must have arrived when we were out."

"Where is Grandpa?" I ask her.

"He left at noon to go play a game of golf with some friends."

"Oh cool," I say.

"Alyson, will you do me a favor and run out to the storage shed?

There is something I need you to grab."

"Sure, what do you want?"

"I think you will know when you see it."

I look at her, completely confused. "Just go," she tells me.

I slowly walk across the yard toward the shed. What the heck am I looking for in a shed? Confused, I reach my hand out for the knob and open it. I see something. Then I scream.

"Oh my god, Matt!" I squeal excitedly. My brother steps out of the dark shed into the day, and I give him a hug. "What are you doing here?"

"I came to deliver your clothes," he says, beaming at me.

"No, really, why are you here?"

"It sounded interesting from our phone conversation, and I have nothing better to do, so I asked Mom and Dad if I could come for the rest of the month."

"And they let you?"

"It took some convincing, but they finally liked the idea of me being here, making sure you don't get into trouble." He winks.

"Ha ha. Very funny. Because you are so much more mature than me." I put my arm around him and ruffle his light brown hair.

"Hey, I'm not the one getting into trouble." He smiles.

"So Grandma and Grandpa let you come?" I ask, changing the subject.

"We were more than happy to see more of our grandchildren," my grandma says, walking toward us.

"Matt, I can't believe you're here!" I beam.

"Me neither," he says.

"Well, let's go inside and you two can get caught up," my grandma says, ushering us toward the porch.

"Is your stuff already here, Matt?"

"Yep. I even unpacked it. I arrived late this morning when you were out, so I've gotten to know the place."

I'm about to reply when I hear my name being called. I turn around to see Marc walking into our drive and toward the porch.

"Good afternoon, Mrs. Henderbell. Hi, Aly!"

"Hello, Marc," my grandma says kindly.

"Marc," I say between gritted teeth, not sure what to do, especially after yesterday. "This is my brother Matt."

"Hi Matt, I'm Marc." He puts his hand out.

"Nice to meet you, Matt," he says as they shake hands.

"Hey, Marc, can I, um…talk to you for a minute…alone?" I ask.

"Sure," he says, obviously having no clue what is coming.

"We will just be inside," my grandma says as she and Matt walk into the house. When I hear the screen door slam behind them, I look at Marc.

"Marc, listen, I'm just going to say this very simply. You seem like a really cool guy, and you are nice and fun to be around, but I didn't come here to like anybody."

"Aly, what are you talking about?"

"I don't have a perfect record like you, Marc, so of course you don't want to like someone like me. Besides, there are other guys in California…"

He looks at me, utterly confused. "Aly, I don't know what Eric told you, but it isn't true."

"I know, but you have no idea what I'm dealing with right now, and I don't need to worry about a guy."

"Aly, this is stupid," Marc says. "I don't understand." His face begins to turn red. "We were just going to hang out, you, me, Eric, and Chloe."

"But it's only a few weeks and then I'll probably never see you again. I wish you could understand, but I can't do it… I'm sorry…" I turn and begin to walk to the door.

"Aly, help me understand," he pleads, perplexed at what has just happened, but this time I don't turn back. I leave Marc Maylore in the driveway, and I feel bad for doing it.

<hr />

The next week goes by both slow and fast. I spend a lot of time with my brother and grandparents, boating, swimming, fishing, and getting to know each other more each day. I spend time with Chloe, talking, paddle boarding, and baking. I also find myself at Mr. Bennett's, playing cards, making him food, or listening to him tell me stories of his life. I enjoy keeping him company, and I enjoy talking with him, but it is also hard to find times when Marc isn't there. I haven't completely shut him out. I mean, I still say hi to him when I see him in the neighborhood or when he's at Chloe's, but I don't make an effort to get to know him more either. I'm just cautious. I'm only up here for a couple more weeks, so what is the use of trying to get to know him anyway?

Every day I feel worse about what I said to him, but whenever I see him around, we act like nothing ever happened. We act like acquaintances, people who don't really know each other. That is a lie though because Marc and I were starting to figure each other out.

Maybe Eric was trying to get back at him for something, embarrass him. After all, I found his envy toward Marc very apparent. Nevertheless, I decide to stay away. I mean, I am only here for a month, and then I have to leave. I do feel slightly lonely though. Marc was so easy to talk to, and yet I only knew him a week.

"So when did you first meet Marc?" I ask Mr. Bennett one day after his afternoon tea. He leans back in his chair and adjusts his glasses.

"I met Marc when he was just a young fellow. I used to take him fishing when he was four. I taught him everything he knows about the lake. I used to joke with his parents that Marc was part fish, because it seemed as if he would never get out of the water. One day I was out for a morning walk when I saw a young boy playing in the rocks on the shore. He was a talkative boy and called me over to show me a stone he found. In fact it was this stone right here." He points to a display case with various objects hanging on the wall. I walk over to it and gently pick up the tiny stone, running my fingers over its smooth silvery surface. I smile and wait for Mr. Bennett to continue his story.

"After that day, Marc would always come by my place to drop off his treasures from the lake. Before I knew it, I was taking him out boating and fishing. Then, when I got too old to leave the house, Marc came to me, to keep me company. He drops by every day he can during the summer and other vacations."

"Well, it sounds like you two have a very special bond." I smile looking into the old man's young eyes.

"He really, truly is a remarkable young man. I have never seen someone so caring, so compassionate."

I smile, picturing the Marc I was just beginning to know.

"Alyson," the old man says, "will you join me for dinner tomorrow evening at six?"

"Of course," I reply.

"Thank you," he says. "It is always so enjoyable to see new faces and have people to talk to."

"I find it very enjoyable to talk to someone too." I smile. "Can I get you anything else?"

He shakes his head. "No, thank you."

"I'll see you tomorrow," I say, preparing to leave.

He smiles at me with his white crooked teeth and I leave the old man staring out the window at the lovely lake, the only place he truly calls home.

—————— ((◦)) ——————

That night I can't sleep. I lie awake for hours tossing and turning. Too many thoughts run through my head, mostly about my life and what I'm going to do with myself. I finally decide to turn my thoughts off and go downstairs to get some water. It is when I am walking down the hallway that I stop and peek through the open door of Matt's room to see the light of his iPod turned on.

"Matt?" I whisper, stepping into the room.

The volume of his music must be low because he instantly replies, "Hey, Aly."

"Are you awake?"

"What does it look like?" he whispers back, pulling the earbuds out of his ears.

"Why are you still up?"

"Can't sleep," he replies.

"Me neither." I sit down on the empty twin bed across from him. We sit in silence for some time.

"Aly, how are you doing here?" he asks me, a serious look on his face.

"I'm doing just fine. I'm trying to forget about it and move on. I'm having no impulses to do anything stupid. I'm still mad though, and I just want Mom and Dad to understand."

"Understand what?"

"You know the answer," I say, looking at the ground. "I'm sick of them making up their own reasoning. They don't want to hear my reasoning as to why I did what I did."

"It wasn't their fault, you know. You have to stop blaming other people and start taking responsibility for your decisions."

I take a deep breath. "I'm just so sick of people telling me what I did wrong, because I know. I know. I'm not an idiot. I'm an honors student, and you know what, I get it. I messed up. I just need people to stop telling me what I did and why I did it, and start telling me what I can do to make myself good again." I pause before continuing. "That's why I like it here, no one knows and if they do, they pretend it didn't happen."

Matt nods.

"Gosh, why can't we just live normal lives? Why can't we just have normal parents?"

"I don't know," Matt whispers.

I stand up to leave. "Thank you for coming, Matt. I really do need someone to keep me grounded."

"I know you do." He smiles.

In the morning, I wake up at 8:27. I guess my grandma must have let me sleep in. I consider going back to sleep, but then I decide to get up anyway. I drag myself from my bed, get dressed, and head downstairs.

Matt is still sleeping and so is my grandpa, which is weird because he is usually up way before seven.

"Good morning!" my grandma says, pouring herself a cup of coffee. "Someone is up early."

"Early?" I ask. "I thought I was supposed to be up by seven."

"Technically you are, but you and Matt were up quite late last night."

"Oh, you heard that?"

She nods. "Not the conversation, just the voices. I decided you deserved a break from getting up at seven."

"Well, thanks."

"You can go back to sleep if you want."

"Thanks, but no thanks. I'm going over to Chloe's. She's always up early."

"Okay, just make sure you only go to her house, and call me if plans change."

"Will do," I say and I give her a quick hug as I run out the door.

Chloe's grandparents kindly let me in. They offer me something to eat, which I decline since I grabbed a protein bar on the way out the door.

"They are upstairs," Chloe's grandma tells me.

"Thanks," I say, and I head up the wooden staircase. What did Mrs. Coleman mean by they? My question is soon answered when I approach Chloe's room and hear several familiar voices.

The door is cracked and I quietly walk up to it and peer in. I see Chloe, Marc, and Eric all sitting around a large desktop computer screen, looking at something.

"That looks like her," Eric says, pointing to something on the screen. When I take a closer look, I instantly recognize the website to be a social media one.

"Really, Eric?" Chloe says.

"Come on, guys, everyone looks at other people's profiles. It's not like we are doing anything bad."

"He's right," Marc says.

"Okay," Chloe says, clicking on the screen. The screen changes to someone's profile page, and I almost try to protest when I see whose page it is, but then I shut myself up, remembering that they don't know I'm here.

They have just opened up *my* profile. Great timing to show up, I think. I see my profile picture. A professionally done photo taken by one of the photographers my mom models for. In the picture, I am sitting on a luxurious leather bench in the middle of a white room. I wear a high-waisted black skirt that falls around my body just above my knees, and a dark shirt. My shoes are shiny gray stiletto heels. My hair, which at the time of the picture was a much darker shade of brown, cascades down in perfect curls above my waist. I miss that hair color, I think, wishing I hadn't dyed it several shades lighter before my trip.

My hands rest on my thighs, and my legs are crossed. My make-up is perfectly done with heavy mascara and light eyeshadow, and I give a slight smile. This is definitely a "glamour shot," and I remember loving this picture so much because it made me look "perfect." It made me look like someone I'm not. It also got 709 "likes" on the site, which was the highest number of likes I had ever gotten on a picture.

"Wow," Marc and Eric say at the same time as Chloe clicks off the photo.

"That really looks like the Aly we know..."

"It was only taken two months ago..." Chloe notes.

Chloe opens up my cover photo, which is another glammed-out photo of my family. A professional photographer took it too. In the photo my parents sit on a Victorian-style couch behind a grand white stone fireplace in our living room. I stand off to one side of the couch, my hand resting on the back. On the other side Matt stands, and in front of him, my ten-year-old brother Jake sits on the arm of the chair. My seven-year-old sister Lily sits in front of the couch, striking a dramatic pose. My parents are dressed to the hilt. Actually, I guess we all are wearing fancy black clothing that looks radiant with the white fireplace. We look so...fake, and I am glad when Chloe clicks off that picture too.

Honestly I have no clue why I still have that picture as my cover photo. I have no desire to show my love for my family on social networking sites. Then I remember I liked the photo so much because it reminded me of a picture the cast of a reality show would take.

For the next several minutes, the three of them scroll through photos of me and friends, vacations, and events. In every picture I am either smiling or showing off some piece of designer clothing. There are pictures of me at beach parties and house parties with my friends and those stereotypical red Solo cups. I look so stupid, I think, looking at the pictures with a different perspective. I need to take them down.

Finally, I decide to confront the people in the room because I cannot bear to keep looking at photos of myself. I take a deep breath. "Hey," I say, acting casual and stepping into the room.

Chloe suddenly freezes, forcing Eric to shut down the computer screen so I can't see what they have been looking at. Marc stands toward the back of the room.

"Hey, Aly..." Chloe says, trying to act natural. "I didn't know you were coming by."

"Oh, well, I just decided to drop in, but if you are busy..."

"No! Not at all!" Chloe says, awkwardly laughing. All three of them stare at me: the girl wearing denim shorts and a T-shirt, no makeup, and whose hair is pulled into a straight ponytail. Obviously I'm not looking as glamorous as the girl in the photos that were just shown.

"Marc and I were just leaving," Eric says, beginning to walk to the door. Marc follows but I don't look at him. "Bye, Chloe, bye Aly," he says.

Alone with Chloe, I just look at her.

"You saw, didn't you?" she asks, looking at the ground.

"Yeah..." I reply.

"Sorry...we were just curious as to what your life in LA was like."

"Don't worry," I reassure, sitting down on her bed. Her room is painted blue with several surfboards and various pictures on the walls. Her bed has tropical floral bedding and faces the closet with white doors. Her desk is pushed up against a window that over-looks the choppy lake. I get the impression she spends a lot of time here, even though she lives in Minneapolis.

"We are always interested in the people we meet," I say, looking out the window.

"LA must be really fun. I mean there are beaches, and famous people, and stores, and apparently really good photographers."

I laugh. "It really is different from here."

"I have always wanted to go surf the California waves. Hey, may-be I could come visit!"

"Yeah!" I smile. "That would be fun!"

I spend the next hour talking to Chloe about LA, making my life over there sound better than it really is.

———— ((◊)) ————

When I leave Chloe's and cut back through her grassy yard to mine, I see my grandma in the driveway talking to a lady. They both look serious, and I slowly walk closer to them so I can hear what they are saying, while staying hidden behind the tall trees.

"Well, have they found any of it yet?" my grandma asks.

"Only my grandmother's old ring. Apparently the thieves dropped it on their way out," the lady replies.

"I am so sorry, Ruth; if there is anything we can do, just let us know."

"We will be just fine," the lady replies. "What sickens me though is that the police said that it had to have been someone local, some-one who knew we were all going to be at the Maylores'. That means it could have been someone we know..."

"I know," my grandma says, looking sad. "Normally Paul and I don't lock our doors at night, but we have been taking extra precautions lately, locking up valuables, not leaving windows open."

"What worries me the most is that they will strike again, and hurt someone else…"

I have heard enough. I cross back over and go in the house the back way.

That evening I go to Mr. Bennett's for dinner. I dress up a little, wearing a skirt and floral shirt, and for once I actually put on makeup. I guess I have missed putting myself together every day. Besides, Mr. Bennett always dresses up when he has company, and I want to show him I care.

I walk over to his house and let myself in. "Hello!" I call down the entry hall.

"Alyson! Please come on back!"

I walk back to the dining room, where I hear the clinking of forks and knives. Apparently Mr. Bennett was going to make dinner tonight, which I hope went okay, because normally he has neighbors do it for him. It's not like he chooses not to cook, because I know he wants to do things on his own with all his heart. He is just getting a little too old to stand and prepare food for long periods of time.

I walk back into the old dining room to find not only Mr. Bennett at the table, but also another figure.

"Marc?" I say, trying not to look shocked, annoyed, and confused.

"Aly…" he replies, turning around.

"I didn't know you were coming…"

"He stopped by shortly after you left yesterday, and you guys seem like pretty good friends, so I invited him." Mr. Bennett smiles, looking proud he managed to bring us together.

"Oh, how kind," I say between clenched teeth. I sit down at the table, trying not to make eye contact with Marc. My goal was to stay away from Marc and just today, alone, he manages to appear everywhere I go.

"Well," Mr. Bennett begins, "I prepared baked potato casserole. It isn't anything fancy, and it's fairly simple and quick to make. I hope it's okay because I haven't cooked in a while."

"I'm sure it will be excellent!" Marc says, picking up the pan and serving some on to all three of our plates. I instantly notice that he has dressed up too, wearing a blue button-up shirt with rolled-up sleeves.

"It looks great!" I say, smiling at Mr. Bennett.

"I'm so glad I could invite you two over for supper. It has been so long since I have had company I could joke around and talk to!" the old man says, looking extremely happy.

"Glad I could come," I reply, taking a bite of the casserole.

"You see," Mr. Bennett continues, "I never had any kids, and my wife passed away, but Marc has always been like my son, and, Aly, the more I get to know you, the more you seem like the perfect daughter."

I smile at the compliment.

We continue to talk the rest of the meal about whatever comes to mind, like sports, the lake, and memories. I talk to Mr. Bennett and say minimal words to Marc. After dinner I scoop some ice cream into bowls, and we sit on the back porch watching the sunset. Marc and I do the dishes, while Mr. Bennett tells us a story about the first fish he caught. Then I decide to go home.

"Good night, Mr. Bennett," I call as I'm leaving.

"Thank you for coming, Alyson!" he calls back.

I walk out onto the drive and prepare to turn the corner onto the street when I hear the door close behind me. I turn to see Marc running toward me. "Aly! Please wait up."

"Marc, I thought I made it clear the other day..."

"You did," he says. "But I just need to talk to you for a minute. Let me give you a ride home." He points to his car, which is pulled into the empty garage.

I shake my head. "I think I can walk four houses up."

He desperately looks at me, "Then let me walk you home."

I sigh. "Fine," I say, and I begin to walk.

"Aly, I know exactly what Eric said to you, about me liking you, but don't worry. I just want to be your friend. Eric misunderstood what I was saying. I know you're only here for a while. I just wanted to hang out. We all make mistakes..."

I stop. His words echo through me and I suddenly realize that Marc is right. We all mess up, but that shouldn't stop us from moving forward... It's not like he even did anything to me in the first place. I just made up my mind to try to avoid him so I didn't have to make friends I would shortly have to leave behind.

"Is everything okay?" he asks.

I start walking again. "Yeah... I'm not here to try to start a relationship, and it's weird if one person feels one way and the other doesn't."

"Aly, I want to talk to you. I want to be friends. Something clicked when I first met you, something I have never experienced with anyone else before. I can't explain it, but it is like I have known you my whole life."

"I know what you mean..." I quietly reply.

"Please trust me," he begs. "I want us to be friends."

We stop in front of my grandparents' cottage. I look up at his tousled hair and nice outfit. Then I look into his deep blue eyes.

"Trust me," he whispers. "Just friends."

"I guess I can try the trust thing again," I say, a slight smile on my face.

His serious face turns into a smiling one. "Good," he says. "My grandpa and your grandpa are going to play golf tomorrow, and I'm going too. If you aren't doing anything, maybe you would like to come."

I laugh. "Sure, but I've never played a game of golf in my life."

"Well, you can always drive the golf cart if you can't figure it out, but I'll show you what to do."

"Okay, I'll go," I reply.

"Good," Marc replies, looking relieved.

"I will see you tomorrow then."

"Yeah!" Marc turns to leave.

I watch him walk away until he disappears behind the trees and onto the dirt road before I go into the house.

CHAPTER 9

"**R**eady to go?" my grandpa asks me.

"Yep!" I reply, carrying my grandma's golf clubs, which I will be using, from the garage to the car. "Matt, are you sure you don't want to go?" I ask my brother, who is sitting on the railing of the porch wearing his swim trunks.

"Nah," he says. "I think we all know I can't golf to save my life. Besides, today I have other plans."

"Like what?"

"Lying in the sun." He grins.

"Well, enjoy yourself," I say sarcastically, preparing to get in the car.

"I will!"

"So where are we going golfing?" I ask my grandpa as he pulls out of the driveway and onto the dirt road.

"Beaver Pond. It is the nicest course around."

"Okay," I say. "Sounds cool enough."

I look down at my outfit. Fortunately, I was able to find all the right attire for the day, borrowing shoes and a skirt from Chloe, and clubs from my grandma. Matt threw a pink polo shirt into the box of my clothes, so I wear that too.

"You look like a professional golfer," my grandpa says.

"Thanks, except I think most people who dress like this actually know how to hit a ball with a club."

"You will be just fine," my grandpa assures me.

He is wrong though. Let's just say that golf isn't my thing. Not only can I not hit the ball, but when I do, it only manages to move several inches. I play the first hole with Marc, his grandpa, and my grandpa, but all I really do is make myself look like a fool. I think my ball moves more when I carry it than when I hit it. Everyone tries to give me tips, like keep your head down and shoulders back, but it doesn't work. Honestly I am pretty sure golf is not a sport one can learn in a single day.

At the second hole I tell everyone to go before me. Marc's grandpa hits, sending the ball far down the lane. Everyone congratulates him. Then my grandpa goes and does the same. Once again he is congratulated. The two of them then head back to their cart to wait for Marc and me to tee off.

"Want to go?" Marc asks.

"I'd rather not..." I reply, looking at the ground.

"Suit yourself." Marc places his white golf ball onto a tee. I step back, allowing him to prepare. He takes a deep breath and looks at the course ahead. He slightly bends his knees and lines the club up with the ball. Then he swings. His club glides smoothly, and briskly comes back down, sending the ball soaring through the air. It surpasses both the balls of our grandpas'. I'm speechless, and I'm pretty sure my jaw drops as I stare at his hit.

Our grandpas applaud from the golf cart, and Marc gives a humble smile.

"Well, you're up," he says to me, adjusting his blue golf hat and making sure his polo is neatly tucked into his khaki shorts.

I shake my head. "I better not..." I say, "especially after what you just did there."

"Oh, come on, Aly, do you think I could hit like that the first day I played golf?"

I sigh and set up my ball. I bend my knees as instructed and try a practice swing, which sends me spinning in a circle and nearly falling to the ground.

Marc laughs. I glare at him. "Aly, you aren't supposed to attack the ball, just gently hit it. It's all in the stroke, not the power."

I just look at him, desperately wanting to give up. "Here," he says, setting his club down and walking toward me, "let's try again."

I adjust the ball on the tee. "Okay," Marc says, standing directly behind me. "Grip the club like this." He shows me and I try to mirror what he does. "Good, now bend your knees like this." I copy him. "There you go." He smiles. "Finally, relax your shoulders." I try. "Good, now keep your head down and on the count of three, you are slowly going to bring your club back and then brush it forward. Okay?"

"Okay," I reply. I take one last look at the overcast sky and green course surrounded by trees.

"One," Marc quietly says, standing next to me and grabbing my club to help me guide it back. "Two." I adjust my feet. "Three," he says, and together we swing the club. I actually hit the ball. It only goes about twenty-five yards, but I am shocked I was able to do something like that.

"See," Marc says, stepping back. "It isn't that hard."

I don't say anything. I just watch my ball slowly roll to a stop.

Suddenly the sky above me flashes, and I look up to see lightning. Then it cracks again, sending a low, loud rumbling over the golf course. Then the rain comes, and it comes in a downpour. I look at Marc, and the two of us run over to the parked golf cart. At that moment a siren sounds, telling people to get off the course. "All right, kids," Mr. Maylore calls, "time to go back."

Marc starts up the cart, and we ride in silence. I watch the rain come down. It pours hard and heavy over the green golf course. A breeze makes the trees sway on both sides of the golf lanes. The sky lights up again, followed by a loud crack of thunder. I shudder at the noise and cross my arms, trying to stay warm and dry. When we pull up at the entrance, we abandon our carts and take refuge inside the check-in room. I look out the window at the empty course being pelted by rain.

Mr. Maylore goes to talk to one of the employees about when we can finish our game, and Marc, my grandpa, and I wait in the corner up against the window.

"Sorry about the weather," my grandpa says, "should have looked at the forecast."

"You didn't check the forecast?" I ask, pulling off my pink golf hat and making sure my half-wet hair is smoothed back in its ponytail.

"Well, normally it's good weather," my grandpa dully replies.

"It's okay, Mr. Henderbell, we can always come back," Marc says. I can't tell if he is disappointed it's raining or if he's glad.

We stand in silence until Mr. Maylore returns. "Okay, so the manager says that the course will reopen a half hour after the lightning stops."

"So, we could be waiting here for a long time..." I say, suddenly bored.

"Yes, unless we decide to go home," my grandpa says. "Personally, I would like to finish my round of golf."

"Me too," Mr. Maylore agrees.

Marc looks at me. "Aly and I could bail. I have my car and Grandpa, you could get a ride home with Mr. Henderbell. Besides, it's like four o'clock and we could go get dinner on the way home."

"Well, Marc, I don't want to ruin your golf game," I say, trying to sound nice, although I really don't want to wait around here for an hour.

"I play this course all the time. Missing out on one game isn't a problem."

"Are you sure?"

"Yeah." He smiles. "Besides, I could go for some food. Is it okay if we go?" Marc asks.

"Fine with me," my grandpa says.

"Yeah, you two go have fun, while us old men stand and wait for the rain to stop." Mr. Maylore chuckles.

"Awesome, thanks!" Marc beams. "Come on Aly, let's go," and he beckons me to follow him to the parking lot.

The rain pours all the way back to Davis Lake. We drive into the small town for dinner and Marc takes me to the bistro where I went with my grandma. The restaurant is fairly empty, due to the weather, and we are given a booth up against a wall of various wine bottles. The overall lighting is dim, and the dark wooden walls and booths don't help lighten up the place. Nevertheless, it seems cozy, especially on a rainy evening. The waitress comes to take our drink order and we both order water. "I don't think you two will need the drink menu." She laughs, grabbing it from the table. "I'll be right back with your waters, kids!" she says, walking off.

The waters come and we order a large platter of nachos, since Marc claims they are the best. Then we wait.

"So what are your plans for the future?" Marc asks me, taking a sip of water.

"How far into the future?"

"Well, what do you want to do with your life after high school?"

I pause, trying to think of my answer. "Honestly, I don't know..." I say. "When I was younger I wanted to get into the whole Hollywood business like my parents, but the older I get, the more I want to avoid fame and fortune."

Marc nods, listening contently to my story. "I mean I want to go to college and get a good job; I just don't know in what field."

"You said you had a 4.0, right?"

"Yeah, all the way through high school, so I shouldn't have a problem getting accepted into a school. I think I'd like to stay somewhere in California."

"What is life like having two famous parents?" he asks, changing the subject.

My smile fades. "Let's just say their life is great for sure. I mean, I get whatever I want, I get to do a lot of cool things I'm truly grateful for, and meet a lot of celebrities and important people, but in terms of my parents as parents, I would say they are a little too absorbed in their own work. Growing up I always had a nanny, and I would only see my parents when they didn't have anything going on. I learned most everything from the nanny, not my mom. The older I got, though, the more independent I became. I think I ask Matt for advice more than I ask my mom and dad. I sound mean, and I know my parents try. It's just I have never clicked with them." I stop, wanting to be done with the conversation. Marc must see that too because he doesn't ask any other questions.

"So what do *you* want to do with your life?" I ask, moving on.

"My parents want me to be a doctor."

"Do you want to be a doctor?"

He shrugs. "I've always kind of had that mindset. My parents have practically laid out a plan of what I need to do to get into the right school and have the right opportunities."

"Well, at least they think about your education and life," I say.

"Yeah, maybe a little too much. They freak out when I don't do well on a test or blow off a study session for basketball or something else. I think if I failed a test, I would be more worried about their disappointment than my own, if that makes any sense."

"Yeah, I get it."

"I mean, I just have so much pressure from them all the time, which puts more pressure on myself. That's why I'm so stressed constantly. I love coming up here because for a few weeks, I don't have to hear my parents constantly nagging about college and my potential life in the medical field..."

"So do you want to be a doctor?" I ask again.

"Didn't I just answer that?" he replies.

"You answered in terms of pleasing your parents, not yourself."

"I honestly don't know. There are definitely some perks, but I'm not sure if I can necessarily see myself in a medical setting..."

"I don't want to screw up what your family has going for you, but you have to do what makes you happy, even if it upsets the people around you. It's your life, not theirs."

He pauses and I can tell he is carefully coming up with a response. "I love basketball and in the short term I know I want to play basketball in college. Several scouts with potential scholarship opportunities have even contacted me..."

"Wow, Marc, scholarships? That's amazing!"

"Yeah," he humbly says, taking another sip of water. "Are you into any sports?" He is obviously directing the conversation away from himself.

"I was a cheerleader, but I quit halfway through the season last year."

"Of course you were." Marc chuckles.

"What is that supposed to mean?"

"You seem like the type of girl who would be into that stuff—on the surface." He winks. "Why did you quit?"

"Life got too hard…" I say.

Then the nachos come. "Enjoy, kids!" The waitress smiles, setting the heaping plate of chips and cheese in front of us.

Marc is right. The nachos are extremely good. They contain the perfect amount of cheese and chips, and it reminds me of the nachos my dad used to make when Matt and I were little, though he hasn't made them in years. Marc and I finish the large plate in between light conversation about boating and plans for the next week.

The waitress comes to collect our finished plate and bring the check. Marc pulls out his credit card, but I protest. "I'll pay," I say, taking out a handful of cash my grandparents gave me. I leave the waitress some money and she goes to get change. When I look back at Marc, he is looking across the restaurant at something. I turn to see Chris and Andrew, who I sort of met at the barbeque. They stand near the entrance of the restaurant. He looks bothered by their presence. "Will you excuse me real quick," he says, looking annoyed.

"I'll just meet you outside," I reply.

"Thanks," Marc says, and he stands up. I watch him walk over to Chris and Andrew. They greet him, but he doesn't give a kind reply. The three leave the restaurant and disappear into the rain.

I get my change and leave a tip. I cross my arms outside the door of the restaurant and look left to right in the blinding rain for Marc. I don't see him, but I choose to go right, toward the car. I pass by the alley next to the restaurant and out of the corner of my eye see several figures moving. I look, and sure enough there stand Marc, Andrew, and Chris. "Fine!" I hear Marc raising his voice. "But just stay away from me!" and then he turns around and angrily begins to walk toward me. His preppy clothes don't seem to match the scene of a dark alley and two kids dressed in light beach wear. When Marc turns away, Andrew and Chris take off running through the rain in the other direction.

"What was that about?" I ask Marc as he hurries through the rain, looking irritated.

"Nothing," he plainly states. He unlocks the car and we both hop in, dripping wet. I don't ask any further questions. Marc doesn't pry into my life and I won't do the same, but I can't help but wonder. I have never seen Marc that angry before.

Marc turns on the radio quietly in the background, and we slowly begin to drive through the suddenly gloomy-feeling town. "Thank you for dinner," he says, composing himself again.

"No problem," I say, running my fingers through my wet ponytail. "Thank you for leaving golf early with me. I don't think it's my calling."

"Hey, you didn't do that bad!" he says, sounding back to his old self.

I smile and lean back in my seat.

We take the long way home, the way that goes all around the lake, since we have nothing better to do. It takes thirty minutes versus the usual ten. It is still raining extremely hard when we get back to our street. Marc slowly drives his car down the dirt road, trying to see what is ahead of him. "It hasn't rained like this in forever..." Marc quietly says. I look out the side mirror, watching the rainfall in the dark green forest. Suddenly I see something unusual.

"Marc! Stop the car!"

"What's going on?" he asks, putting the car in park.

"Do those look like people crossing the street back there?" I whisper.

He nods. "But who would be out in this kind of weather?"

I turn and look at the figures in the distance. There are two of them, and I can make out a large sack in one's hand. Then it hits me. The robbers.

"Marc, unlock the doors!"

"What? No!"

I end up doing it myself. I push open the door and run into the rain. "Aly!" Marc yells, but I start running toward the figures. They must see me because the second I get out of the car, they break out running toward the forest. "Hey!" I yell at them. "Get back here!"

---

and I sprint toward the trees, leaving Marc in his car in the rain.

The mud from the dirt road cakes my feet and legs. As far as I know, they could be men or teenagers. Obviously, they want to look like the stereotypical thieves. Rain pelts my face in sheets, but I run forward, determined to catch these robbing idiots. I dart into the trees and dodge the logs, trunks, and thick green underbrush. The good thing is that I can still see them ahead of me running like maniacs. One keeps looking back every several yards, seeing if I am still on their tail. The one carrying the bag never turns around. They both wear black hoodies with the hoods pulled up, and black masks cover their faces.

The further into the forest I go, the thicker it becomes. I have to start looking at my feet, trying to step in between the fallen sticks and tangled, lush plants. I can't run in a straight path because every couple of feet or so there is a tree, making it hard to catch up with them.

I look up at the canopy of trees above me. The light green leaves clash with the dark sky, and water rolls from the diamond-shaped leaves in thick drops, hitting my head. I look up ahead again to see that I'm gaining on them. I can hear their panting and heavy breaths ahead of me. I'm pretty sure they are scared by my attempt to chase them down. "Faster!" I hear one say to the other between breaths. I can't recognize the voice, and I don't think I ever would be able to with how heavy he is breathing.

The chase continues, and I start to get winded. The unruly underbrush becomes even harder to run through, if that is even possible. Bushes and various twigs scratch my body as I brush past, and I shudder as I feel a stick cut my leg, sending a warm trickle of blood down my ankle.

"Hurry!" the same guy says again. I laugh to myself. At the rate these guys are running, I will catch them soon enough.

And then something happens. I misjudge where a branch is and I trip, sending my body crashing to the ground. I hit my head on a log and then everything goes black.

When I wake up, I find myself lying on a soft bed or couch, but I'm still wet. I hear muffled voices around me, though I don't concentrate on what they are saying. I'm more preoccupied with a throbbing headache. I crack my eyelids open and am instantly blinded by a bright light. I'm definitely not in the rainy, dark forest anymore.

I then finally decide to open my eyes, forcing light into them. When I open them, I instantly recognize the wooden ceiling of my grandparents' house. I'm home. But how? I decide to sit up, but when I put weight on my left arm, I feel a light pain and soreness. I look over to find bloodstained gauze below my shoulder. I must have cut it while falling down. And then it all comes rushing back—Marc, the robber, my chase, my fall. My fall. That is why I'm here. I blacked out.

My grandma, who is talking to someone in the corner, looks back at me and sees I'm awake. "Alyson!" she says, sounding relived. She rushes to my side. "Are you okay, honey? Talk to me!"

"Grandma, I'm fine," I calmly say.

She doesn't look convinced. The man she was talking to walks over beside her and looks at me. "Hi, Alyson." He smiles. "I'm Dr. Meyers. I live down the street. I'm here to make sure you're okay."

"Oh, I'm fine," I say, trying to stand up, but I feel slightly dizzy. My grandma pushes me back down.

"Not so fast," Dr. Meyers says. "I just need to run some quick tests on you to make sure you don't have a concussion or other major injuries."

"Was my fall that bad?" I question, trying to remember.

"Well, you were found collapsed in the forest with your head resting on a log." Dr. Meyers shines a light in my eyes. "You hit your head. I'm surprised it hasn't begun to swell."

"Who found me?"

"Marc," my grandma says, putting her hand on my shoulder.

That makes sense. He did watch me take off into the woods. "Where is he now? Did you catch the robbers?"

"Alyson, calm yourself," my grandma says. "You will have plenty of time to get the answers to your questions, but the robbers were not caught. In fact they weren't anywhere near you when Marc showed up."

"And Marc?" I ask.

"I'm pretty sure he is outside with everyone else waiting. No one is allowed in the house right now."

"Everyone?"

"Your brother, your grandpa, Marc, his family, Chloe's family, and several other neighbors, and the police."

"Am I in trouble?"

She shakes her head. "No, but they do want to talk to you when you are well enough."

"I want to talk to Marc," I say.

"You will." My grandma smiles.

"Well," Dr. Meyers begins, "you seem very talkative, which is a good sign. Your body seems fine, other than the gash down your arm, which we will tend to. I'm going to ask you a couple of questions first, to see if there is any initial sign of a concussion." I easily answer the questions he asks. "Good, good!" Dr. Meyers exclaims. "You seem well enough, but I will need you to come in tomorrow for more thorough tests."

I nod. "Thank you."

He and my grandma go off into the other room. I am left alone on the couch. It's now that I start thinking about the robbery. Whose house did they hit this time? And why? Surely with the precautions that our street has been taking, they would have known not to come back, but I guess not. The voices of my grandma and Dr. Meyer have disappeared. I wonder why, but right as I'm about to call out to them, Marc walks into the living room.

He looks horrible, drenched from head to toe with rainwater, and his legs and shorts are covered in mud and grass. His hands are also caked with mud, and his shirt has various dirty spots on it.

I have just ruined his preppy golf outfit. I see blood trickling down his legs in several places where he must have been scratched while running through the forest.

The appearance of Marc draws me to look down at myself. I knew I was wet, but I look just as bad, if not worse than Marc with all the mud and dirt covering my body from head to toe. I'm suddenly embarrassed. He smiles when he sees me. "Hey, you don't look half bad!"

I laugh dryly. "Don't pretend I don't look like a wreck."

"We can both look like wrecks together," Marc says, walking toward me. I notice his clean bare feet. He must have removed his shoes before entering the house.

"So how are you feeling?" he asks.

"Fine," I reply. "I kind of have a headache, but the doctor says it doesn't look like I have a concussion."

"Good!" Marc says. "I was worried when I found you. Especially the way your head was resting on the log."

"How did you find me?"

"Well, the moment you bolted from the car like a maniac, I ran after you, but only after I dialed 911. Then I ran and let the phone ring. I knew they would come to trace the call. Since I knew the police were coming soon to deal with the burglars, I followed you. I wasn't far behind. I saw you fall. Then when I saw you had passed out, I panicked, but I managed to half drag, half carry you to the road where the cops were waiting. Dr. Meyer showed up, and well, you know the rest."

"Thank you," I reply.

"Sorry I couldn't have done more..."

"More?" I just look at him. "You saved me. If you hadn't come after me, I would probably still be in the forest. I'm sorry I dragged you into this..."

"Well, I guess we're even then."

"Marc, you did nothing worth apologizing for."

He doesn't look convinced.

Once all the commotion has died down and everyone has left,

I take a shower. I stand there in the hot water, letting all the mud, dirt, and blood run down my body into the drain. I take a long shower and use as much soap as I possibly can. When I'm warm, clean, and ready for bed, my grandma tends to my arm, putting some thick goo on it and then wrapping it with a fresh bandage. I take some pain medicine for my headache and go to bed. The moment my head hits the pillow, I fall asleep.

CHAPTER 10

The beat of the song drops, making the music even louder. The bass shakes the room. Around me lights flash in many colors and patterns. There are people everywhere, some dancing, some obnoxiously talking and laughing. I can't quite make out their faces though. I am wearing a sparkly dress that shines silver and blue in the lights, and my hair falls above my waist in perfect curls.

In the back corner of the party scene, I see someone looking at me. I don't recognize him because he is wearing a dark hoodie that covers his face. He motions me to come to him. Reluctantly, I leave the dancing crowd and make my way toward him. He hands me a rolled-up paper bag and then strolls away into the crowd. I open it. Inside I see a silver clutch with a price tag on it: one hundred billion dollars. Scribbled under that is a handwritten note that reads, don't get caught.

I put it back in and casually begin to walk away, although my heart is pounding. Where did this come from?

Suddenly someone taps me on the shoulder. I quickly turn around to see my mom and two cops standing behind her. She looks at me. Her face shows no emotion, yet I can tell she is disappointed. "What are you doing, Alyson? Why do you have that? How did you get that?" she asks.

I try to open my mouth to speak, but no words come out. She just stands there tapping her foot, looking annoyed and waiting for a response that never comes. Moments pass as she stares me down, and then with no explanation she rips the bag from my hand and slides out the clutch. "Officers," my mom plainly calls, "arrest her. She's the robber." I panic and try to cry out. I try to tell her she has no right to arrest me and that the bag isn't mine. I am no robber. But once again my voice doesn't work.

The scene fades, and I find myself at my house in LA, standing in the foyer. The grand marble staircase is off to one side, the white wooden entry doors behind me. Above me, peeking from behind a pole upstairs so they cannot be seen, my two brothers watch. My parents stand in front of me. They both look tired. My dad wears jeans and a gray shirt, still holding the car keys in his hand. He looks at me, for I think he has already said what he has to say. My mom wears a black party dress, like she has just gotten home from an event. I know this scene all too well.

I'm no longer wearing my sparkly dress—just my muddy golf clothes from earlier. My face is tear streaked and smeared with makeup. I am crying, hard. Both my parents yell at me, demanding answers, but I still can't talk. All I can do is cry. "We are extremely disappointed," they say.

It takes all my energy to speak. "I'm sorry!" I scream and then I sit up in bed.

My room is dark. I am sweating, and crying. My head no longer hurts, but the cut in my arm slightly stings and feels burning hot from being under the covers. I am breathing heavily. "I'm sorry," I whisper again, trying to catch my breath.

Right then, my grandma opens the door. "Alyson, honey, are you okay?" she whispers.

I want to say yes. I want to say I am fine, like I always say, but I say nothing.

She walks into my dark room and sits at the end of my bed. "Did you have a bad dream?"

I nod, sniffling. Then I wipe my eyes with my hands. "I screamed, didn't I?" I ask, my voice trembling so that is barely a whisper, but I know the answer. "I'm sorry I woke you..."

"Oh, don't be sorry," my grandma says, reaching for a box of tissues and handing me one. "What happened in the dream?"

I don't know how to respond. I take a deep breath, trying to compose myself. "I relived my own nightmare...at least part of it." I say, tears beginning to run down my face again.

My grandma looks at me. I can tell she feels sorry. Her look says it all.

"Grandma," I slowly say, making my voice more apparent. "I messed up. I messed up a lot. I know that now. The problem is when I try to get over it, it just gets shoved right back in my face. It haunts me. Everything I think about, everything I do. I was stupid. Immature. Everything my parents said was right. I should have just behaved. I shouldn't have tried to rebel. At the time, I had my own motives. I wanted attention. I wanted to be heard. You have to believe me. I never meant to upset anyone, not even myself."

"Alyson, I believe you. We all make mistakes."

"Am I a bad person?"

She shakes her head. "A bad person wouldn't recognize and accept that they made a mistake." I look down at the bedspread. "You are only lost, unsure what to do."

"But if I'm not a bad person, why do I feel like one?"

"Guilt, disappointment, loss. Those are all things we feel when we mess up," she tells me.

"But how do I move forward without this dictating my life? I mean, I'm pretty sure my parents will be hesitant every time I ask to leave the house for the rest of my life."

"Alyson, moments in life define us, but it is our choice as to who we become."

Her words sink in hard, and I can't stop thinking about them.

"Everything is going to be okay. You just need to think about what you want in your life. Mistakes happen, but we learn."

"Will you stay with me until I fall back asleep?" I ask, feeling like a little kid again.

She smiles. "Of course, dear."

I lie back down and take a deep breath, closing my eyes. I feel my grandma pull the covers up. I fall asleep before I can even thank her for what she has said.

"Whose house was it?" I ask Chloe the next afternoon. The two of us sit on her wooden dock, dangling our feet into the crisp, choppy water.

"The Pearsons'," she replies. "They had just left to go back to their main home in Chicago."

Her blonde wavy hair is pulled up into a high ponytail, and she wears white shorts and an oversized T-shirt over her swimsuit. She looks worried.

"What was taken?" I ask, trying to get caught up on what occurred the night before, since I was sort of preoccupied.

"Well, some family heirlooms, like some ancient coins or something, and artifacts from the Civil War, along with some old jewelry and a little bit of cash."

"Wow…" I say, speechless at how unkind some people in this world are.

"I know," she quietly replies. "I wonder who's next?"

I spent my morning at the doctor's office in the next town over. They ran countless tests on me, to confirm I didn't have a concussion, which I was thankful about. Then I went back to town to visit the police station, where I was questioned about the crime. I gave them all the information I had, which sadly wasn't much. Then I went home to find Chloe sitting alone on her dock.

"Well, hopefully they will catch them soon. I mean, they know it has to be someone local," I say.

"How local?" Chloe asks. "This lake is huge."

"Beats me," I reply, watching a Jet Ski gliding across the choppy waters. I wonder if it is Marc or Eric.

"Are you going to be here for the Fourth of July?" Chloe asks, changing the subject.

"Matt and I are supposed to leave the first," I say, surprised I have almost been up here for a full month. The time has flown.

"Oh," Chloe says, looking down and sounding disappointed. "You're going to miss out on a great firework show."

I force a smile on my face. "I don't want to go either."

I can't believe those words have just come out of my mouth. I never once thought in a million years I would want to stay, but the closer I get to having to go home, the more I don't want to.

"I'm going to miss you, Aly," she says. "It has been forever since there has been another girl to hang out with here. Normally it's just me, Marc, and Eric."

"Yeah, it's weird to have to go home..."

"But I bet you miss your parents, right?"

"You have no idea," I casually say. And right then the thought of going home sinks in—the thought of having to return to my once normal life, my once normal friends, and my once normal behaviors. I can't go.

"Chloe, will you excuse me?" I ask, standing up. "There's something I have to do."

And with that, I run back across the dock up the hill, through Chloe's yard, and into my yard. I run into the house. "Where's Matt?" I ask my grandpa.

"Um, I think he went upstairs to change out of his swimsuit."

"Thanks," I yell as I dart up the stairs.

"Matt! Matt!" I shout as I run into his room.

"God, Aly, what happened to knocking? I could have been changing!"

"Sorry, sorry!" I say, panting. "I need to ask you something."

"What?" he asks, annoyed.

"Are you bored here?"

"No." He looks confused.

"Do you find it fun here?"

"Yeah I do. Why?"

"Matt, I don't want to leave in two days. I want to stay."

My grandparents, Matt, and I sit at the long dining room table, Matt and I on one side, my grandparents on the other. The house phone sits between us, resting on the surface of the shiny wood.

My grandma looks at us. "Like we said, all you have to do is make the call."

I want to argue, but I know it's no use.

"I can do it if you want, Aly," Matt generously says.

My grandma and grandpa ignore him and stare at me, for I'm the one who needs to call.

"Okay," I sigh, "I'll do it."

My grandma hands me the phone, and I dial the number I've known for so long. The phone begins to ring. Please go to voicemail, please go to voicemail and make this easy, but as I suspect the phone is answered.

"Hello, this is Cassidy Butler," the voice says, sounding occupied.

"Hi Mom," I say, trying to sound excited and happy, although I'm pretty sure I sound annoyed and sarcastic.

"Alyson!" my mom gushes, sounding shocked that I've actually called her. "You called!"

"I did," I say in the same tone of voice as before.

"How's everything in Minnesota?" she asks, trying to sound motherly and polite.

"Good. Really good."

"Are you treating your grandparents with respect?"

I roll my eyes, even though she can't see me. "Yes, Mom," I say between clenched teeth.

"So, I'm assuming you are learning your lesson."

I cut her off. "I'm not calling for your lectures," I say, raising my voice. Then I see my grandma's face, and I force myself to calm down.

"Why are you calling?"

I laugh dryly. "I just wanted to tell you that Matt and I will be spending some more time up here this summer. Grandma and Grandpa are fine with it. I'm not quite sure of the date we will be returning, but we will let you know when we get our flight changed."

I hear a pause on the other line and then some talking. "Oh, Alyson, that's great!" my mom replies, sounding distracted. I hear another pause and some more talking. "Thank you so much for telling me. You know what, I have to scoot, but tell your grandmother that I'll call her later. Thanks for calling. Sorry I can't talk more."

"That's fine by me, Mom," I reply in a tone that sounds harsher than I intended. Then I hang up.

I set the phone down and look up. Three pairs of eyes stare at me. "She said she was fine with it. She sounded thrilled. She will also be calling you later to talk," I say to my grandma, still annoyed.

"Yes!" Matt breathes, sounding relieved.

"Thank you for letting us stay." I smile, my voice finally sounding normal again.

—————•《◊》•—————

Matt and I walk down to Marc's later to tell him the good news. When we arrive at his house, we find Marc and Eric playing basketball in the driveway. Chloe sits on the porch steps watching. *Good,* I think. *I can tell everyone at once.*

"Hey!" Marc smiles as we walk into the drive.

"Hey, Marc." Matt walks up the driveway to join the game.

"Hi." I sit down by Chloe. Basketball isn't my sport.

The game starts up again. Eric takes a shot and asks how I'm feeling.

"Good," I reply. "The doctor says there are no signs of a concussion. I just have to wait for my cuts to heal." The thought of cuts makes me think of Marc, and I look down at his legs to see various red scratches weaving up and down the leg. Some even have Band-Aids. Part of me thinks his scratches are worse than mine, and he didn't even do anything.

"I can't believe you did that." Eric chuckles. "I mean who does that?"

"Does what?" I question.

"Chases robbers through a forest."

I don't reply. I force a smile and then I laugh at myself. It sounds kind of stupid now that I think of it.

"Hey, at least you don't have a concussion. It would suck to spend your last two days here not feeling well."

"That's actually why I came by," I say. Marc, who is in mid-jump of taking a shot, stops and looks at me. Eric turns too, and so does Chloe. "Matt and I are going to spend some more time here."

"Really?" Chloe asks.

"Yep! Got it all sorted out today," Matt says.

"Yay! You guys will be here for the Fourth of July then!" Chloe beams. Eric happily nods, and when I look at Marc, he's casually smiling, although I know he is only acting calm and humble in front of us. I get the feeling that on the inside, he is excited about the news. Acting calm is just a Marc thing.

The guys find it hard to play a game with three, and after a while they begin a shooting drill to see who can make the most shots from a certain point. Naturally, Marc and Eric, being seniors on Varsity Basketball, beat my brother, by a lot, but the score is close between Marc and Eric. I can tell both are very competitive.

It is Marc's turn and he stands directly behind the line and shoots. The ball hits the backboard and swooshes through the net. Point for Marc. He cheers victoriously, and laughs. Chloe and I cheer too. "All right, Eric, you're up," Marc states, giving Eric the ball and stepping back. Eric positions the ball and shoots. It doesn't even hit the backboard. It just glides perfectly through the net. Eric's face lights up. He has finally tied with Marc.

"Wait, Eric." Marc calmly steps up by his friend. "You were in front of the line when you shot."

Eric, who hasn't really moved since his last shot, looks at his feet. Marc is right. Eric is in front of the line. "Come on, man, it was a nice shot," he pleads.

"But if Coach were here he would say..."

Eric doesn't let him finish. "Shut up! Shut up!"

Marc cautiously steps back, dropping the basketball. It bounces off the driveway into the yard.

"Coach isn't here! Looks like perfect little Marc can't let his friend do better than him for once in his life. My shot was obviously better, but you can't allow yourself to accept the fact that you are not always the best."

Marc looks confused. "No, I was just trying to tell you..." but once again he doesn't get to finish.

"Stop man! For once let me take pride in myself for doing something right!"

"Eric," Marc calmly says. "Don't get so worked up; it is just a game of shooting."

"Really? Then don't get yourself so worked up about where someone shoots from."

"I was just pointing out the line... What's the big deal?"

"What's the big deal?" Eric taunts, and then out of nowhere, he curls his fist and punches Marc as hard as he can in the face.

Chloe screams. Matt steps back. I jump to my feet. Marc stumbles backward and falls on the hard pavement. He slowly looks up at Eric, who holds his trembling fist and looks scared and shocked. Blood begins to trickle from Marc's lip, and within seconds his cheek swells with a reddish blue color. Eric breathes heavily and his face is bright red. I also see tears welling in his eyes. The two stare at each other for what seems like hours. Marc moves and I see him trying to stand up. I run to help him, but he pushes me away. "I'm fine," he hisses. Obviously, he feels disoriented, for it seems to take him quite a few seconds to stand. When he gets to his feet, he takes a step toward the now weak Eric. Eric steps back and for a second I fear Marc will punch him back. He doesn't. Instead he just walks to up to Eric. "Oh, I see how it is now," he growls in his face. "I see how it has always been."

And then he pushes Eric away. Eric stumbles and falls in the grass. He looks up at Marc like a scared child.

Marc glares at Eric one more time and then he turns and runs toward his car. "Marc, wait!" I yell, but he doesn't look back. He gets in his car and speeds out of the driveway, bringing up dust from the dirt road and leaving the four of us standing there speechless.

————))(((————

"Have you talked to Eric?" I ask Marc three days later. The two of us stand on the town's public docks. A thick layer of fog covers the water, making it impossible to see across the lake. The clouds are gray and dark, giving the whole area an eerie feel.

Marc looks down at the churning gray water hitting the dock down below. "He came to apologize that night."

"And?"

"And what, Aly?" he snaps, still angered by the whole experience. "I accepted his apology. I felt so guilty about the way I acted, I had no choice. We talked things through. We're fine."

"Really?" I ask. "You don't seem fine."

He looks up at me. The swelling on his cheek has gone down, but a purple bruise is still present. His deep blue eyes, always so full of life, look sad, hurt, betrayed. "I just never thought Eric would do something like that to me. I thought we were better than that. I thought we could talk, and trust each other. I guess I was wrong, because he never once told me he felt jealousy... ever. You don't understand, Aly. He's always been my best friend. We have done everything together. I can't lose him, though I fear I already have. Things will never be the same."

"I'm not one for giving advice about friendship," I quietly begin, "but I do know one thing—mistakes happen. They happen all the time whether we want them to or not. If you feel like you can't lose Eric, then you can't lose Eric. You have to go with your gut feeling. There are very few people who come into our lives and make an impact, and I'm pretty sure Eric has made a big impact on you. You need to talk to him again. Tell him how you feel. Figure out what went wrong and go from there. Start again if need be." I pause. Marc looks away from me.

"Marc, please make things right. I can't tell you how many relationships with friends and family I've messed up. And I will tell you this; if they are not initially fixed, they never will be. Don't spend the rest of your life regretting not making this right. You want to. He wants to. I know he does. So please go talk to him."

Marc doesn't reply. He just continues to look down at the gray water. Lightning cracks and thunder rumbles across the water, drowning the sound out. It begins to rain. I walk back up the dock, leaving Marc standing alone in the rain.

I go to check on him later that afternoon. Just to see if he actually went to talk to Eric. The rain has stopped, but it's still cloudy. I knock on the door and wait for someone to answer. It takes a while, but eventually I hear footsteps behind the walls of the house. Scott answers.

"Hey, Aly!" he says, eating a sandwich.

"Hi, Scott, is Marc home?"

"No, sorry, he went into town with my grandparents to pick up a couple things at the store. He should be back soon though."

"Oh, I'll just come back another time. I didn't mean to bother you," I say, turning to go.

"No, come in! I insist. Besides, it will give me a chance to talk to the girl my brother spends all his time with."

"You sure?"

He holds the door open and motions me to come in. I follow him into the kitchen. He sits down at the counter and continues to eat his sandwich. He asks me some basic questions about my life and I answer them.

"So Marc says you're in college. Where do you go?" I ask.

"Oregon. I wanted to get as far away from Minnesota as I could.

I do like visiting here in the summer though."

"What are you majoring in?"

"I'm getting my degree in environmental biology, but I want to be a personal trainer."

"Oh," I reply. "So your parents didn't want you to follow in their footsteps and become a doctor?"

"They lost hope in me at a young age. They knew I would never make it through med school, let alone get into med school. They put their faith in Marc. He is the 'Mr. Perfect Know It All' in our family."

"Does that bother you?"

"Nope! Marc is going to be the successful, smart one. We all know that. It takes a hell of a lot of pressure off me. My parents are relieved I, a) got into a decent school and b) haven't flunked out yet." He laughs.

"Well, good for you..." I say, not quite sure how to reply.

Suddenly I hear a door open and people entering the house. "Don't you understand? I don't want to go to a stupid medical school convention!" Marc says, raising his voice. "I don't need old guys telling me about possible opportunities. I know my opportunities. My mom and dad have only told me like one hundred times. I've looked at colleges, I have met with a planner, I'm fine. Besides they told me they wouldn't bother me with thoughts of school this summer."

"Marc, are you sure you..." his grandma begins, but he cuts her off.

"Tell them I'm not going." Their footsteps are getting closer to the kitchen. "Sometimes I wish I would have just told them I was never going to be a doctor... I was never going to be like them..." Marc mutters.

Scott sticks his head out into the hallway. "I would hate to rain on your little conversation, but before you guys all start expressing how you really feel about a medical school convention, you might want to know we have a guest."

The discussion in the hallway completely stops. Scott casually strolls back into the kitchen and goes over to the fridge. Marc follows him, and when he sees it's me, his face turns red.

"Hello, Alyson." Mrs. Maylore beams, walking into the kitchen.

"If this isn't a good time, I can come back later," I tell her.

Before she can reply, Marc says, "No! You picked a great time to come. Come on, Aly, let's go upstairs. I can tell you about the Fourth of July plans."

I reluctantly follow Marc up the stairs and into his room.

"Are you okay?" I ask when we are alone.

He nods. "I'm fine, just a normal disagreement about college."

"Normal?"

"My parents always want to send me to stuff like that. I wish they would just understand I don't want to go."

"Marc, have you ever talked to them about...you know, maybe giving you some space to figure out your own career path? It sounds like that's what they did with Scott..."

"Scott was a different story. In their eyes he was never 'doctor material'. Aly, it's fine, really. I'm overreacting. You probably think my parents are crazy control freaks. They just want the best for me, and sometimes I forget they are only trying to give me the best life possible."

I smile and almost wish my parents were so picky about my future.

"I know they put pressure on me, but without it I probably wouldn't be motivated to do well in school." He laughs. "I would be like Scott."

"So you are good?"

"Yeah." He pauses, and a smile forms on his face. "Now let me tell you about what we are going to do on the Fourth!"

<hr/>

The Fourth of July comes, and it's a blast. My grandparents host a barbeque in our backyard. The trees and tables are decked out in red, white, and blue. Everyone on our street brings something. There is music, dancing, fun, and games.

I guess Marc and Eric worked things out because they act as if the fight never happened. After the barbeque, once the sun has dropped, everyone prepares to watch the fireworks. They line up lawn chairs along the shore. However, Marc and Eric decide we should view the fireworks another way.

Marc asks to borrow my grandpa's speedboat, and he allows him to use it. Chloe, Eric, Matt, Marc, and I stay out on the lake until midnight, watching fireworks burst with color around us. I've always loved watching fireworks. There is something about the way everything is completely silent and then an instant later, the sky explodes with both noise and color. Everyone seems happy during the fireworks. Everyone seems to forget about, well, life and just focus on the present. From the middle of the lake, we can see every grand sparkle of color reflect on the water like a mirror. The night is perfect.

When we return to the shore, Marc calls after me as I walk along the dock in dark night. "Hey, Aly! Can I ask you something?"

"Shoot," I reply, carrying a pile of towels.

"How would you feel about having dinner with me tomorrow? Just us."

I pause a moment before I reply. I have dined with Marc before, but this feels different. Part of me says I should say no, spare all possibility of it being awkward. But part of me wants to say yes. Wants to say it sounds fun. That part overrules the doubt.

"I would love to." I smile.

As I curl my hair in my room the next day, I play through the conversation in my head. I see him taking me aside on the dock. The others go ahead with the life vests and empty soda cans. "Come on, Aly, just for fun," he says. "Just to talk." I guess we haven't talked in a while, just one on one anyway. So I say yes. There is something about talking to Marc. He listens and always makes me feel better.

I check the time on the old clock hanging on the wall. Ten 'til seven. Marc told me to meet him at his place at seven, so I need to get going. I decide to wear a white lacy sundress. It is one of the nicer pieces I have brought, and it is probably one of the only nights I will get to wear it. I have curled my hair and pulled some of it back. Simple sandals accompany my outfit. I hope it's not too dressy.

I walk down to Marc's, listening to the birds chirp in the green canopy above me. I see the tree limbs sway in the slight breeze. From the road I can hear the faint noise of the lapping lake in the distance. The evening is so peaceful, so calm. And that is one of the reasons I love it here.

I pass by Dr. Meyer's house, then Mr. Bennett's, and finally I arrive at Marc's at the end of the street. I take a deep breath before approaching the home. When I walk toward the front door, I notice something strange. Eric sits on the front porch steps. It looks as if he is waiting for me.

"Eric?" I question, utterly confused. I thought Marc said it was only us for dinner. Maybe I was wrong.

"Hey, Aly," he says, standing up.

"What are you doing here?"

"I'm your escort to dinner."

"But Marc said to come here."

"Yeah, he said to come here. That doesn't necessarily mean you're eating here. Now follow me." He walks toward the side of the house. I begin to follow, but he suddenly stops. "Oh, and you will need this," he says, handing me a life jacket.

"You're kidding, right?" I ask, holding up the life vest and looking at my nice dress. "We have to go out onto the water?"

"Yep," Eric replies, grinning.

He helps me onto the Jet Ski and then lowers it. He hops on and starts up the engine. The water is calm tonight, and I'm glad because my goal here is not to get wet. Eric cautiously drives the Jet Ski out into the middle of the lake. It is then that I notice a small fishing boat bobbing up and down in our wake. Eric idles toward it and pulls up alongside the small boat. I see Marc sitting in the middle of the fishing boat. He smiles when he sees me.

I finally realize the fishing boat Marc's family has wasn't on its lift at the house. I now know why. He has taken out the seats and fishing equipment, and replaced the bottom of the boat with a picnic blanket. On top of that he has placed a smaller checked blanket to serve as the table. Fake candles glow in the center.

Eric helps me off. "Here you go, Aly! You two have fun now!" He winks as he starts up the Jet Ski and drives away.

I look at Marc. "I didn't know this is what you meant by having dinner..."

"Surprise!" He smiles awkwardly. The boat slowly rocks back and forth. We sit down on either side of the candles.

"You look nice," he says quietly.

"Thanks, as do you," I reply, looking at his navy blue button-up shirt with rolled-up sleeves.

"Okay, here are the drinks," he says, reaching into a side compartment and handing me a cold soda.

"Cheers," I say, opening the can.

"To an awesome summer," Marc finishes. We hold the soda can up toward the blue sky.

For the first course Marc has prepared a salad, complete with a basket of bread. Fine dining out on the lake. For the main course we have chicken and potatoes that Marc has somehow kept nice and warm. I eat the tasty meal with satisfaction. If this was an hour ago, I would have thought eating on the bottom of a fishing boat would be impossible. The further we get into our meal, the more I begin to change my mind.

After we eat, Marc clears the plates, food, and candles and stores them in a side compartment. Full, I lie back up against the side of the boat and stretch my legs out. We sit in silence, just enjoying each other's company. I look at Marc, his golden brown hair swished perfectly over his eyebrows, and his blue eyes glimmering like the water, looking content. "Hey!" I suddenly say, excitement rising in my voice. "Your face. It's almost back to normal." The once swollen bruise has faded to a small red spot under his eye.

He nods. "Indeed it is... Aly, I just want to thank you for the advice you gave me the other day. It really meant a lot. After you left, I went back to Eric's. We sorted it all out. We are actually good now."

"That's great!" I smile, glad things are back to normal.

"I also should be thanking you for a lot of things. You have taught me many valuable lessons this summer."

"I have?" I lightly laugh, mildly shocked.

"Yeah, I mean I know you might not think so because your life is so simple, but you have."

"Oh, but my life isn't simple," I say quietly.

"Yes, well, how many times have you messed up, like really bad?"

I pause, letting a bazillion answers to his questions run through my head. But I can't tell him. Not right now. He can't know why I'm really here.

"See," Marc says, "simple, and knowledgeable."

"Yeah," I lie quietly. "Hey, do you have any music?" I ask, changing the subject again.

He nods. "Actually I do. I have my phone." He pulls it out of a compartment and turns it on.

A slow song with a light beat begins playing. "Alyson Butler." He stands up and sticks his hand out. "Would you care to join me for a dance?"

"I would be delighted, Marc Maylore."

He pulls me up and puts his hands on my waist. I put mine on his shoulders. The boat is small, but we manage to go back and forth in little circles. He even twirls me around several times.

"I didn't know you could dance," I say, laughing.

"I can't..."

The song plays on and we do a fairly good job of keeping to the beat, although neither of us are very good dancers. We laugh through most of the song.

The song ends. The two of us stand still, looking into each other's eyes. "That was fun," I whisper.

He nods. "But you have to go for one more turn!" He takes his hands off my waist to twirl me.

"Okay!" I reply, laughing a little too hard. I go out for the turn and begin to spin in the small boat, but then something happens. Something I should have known would happen all along. I stumble and lose my balance, and then it all happens so fast. I begin to fall over. I scream and try to grab Marc for support, but that doesn't help. The two of us go over the side of the boat and into the clear evening water.

I come up from the water drenched. I should be crying out in disappointment, since I have probably just ruined my dry-clean-only dress. But I can't help but laugh as I run my fingers through my straight wet hair.

Marc comes up too, and when he sees I'm amused, he can't help but laugh too. "Aly, not fair, you just got me all wet." He splashes me in the face.

"Sorry," I say, splashing him back, "this is what you get for pulling me into the water that first day."

"Okay, we're even now!"

The two of us, sopping wet, climb back into the perfectly dry fishing boat. Then we sit next to each other and watch the sunset. The ball of fire drops below the horizon, sending swirls of pinks and reds through the vibrant sky. Then we head back to shore, enjoying each other's company.

When we pull in to the dock, I see Eric up at the house sitting on a lawn chair. He must have been waiting for us to return. He stands up and walks toward us.

"Thanks for dinner," I say, stepping out of the boat, still wet. "Sorry about all of this though." I look at his dripping wet outfit.

"No problem." Marc chuckles. "I had a good time."

Eric reaches the dock, and when he nears us, he stops. "What happened to you?" he asks, raising an eyebrow.

"Don't ask," I reply, laughing.

CHAPTER 11

The following evening, after dinner, Matt and I sit on the front porch of my grandparents' house. The sky above us is darkening fast, and I can almost guarantee that there will be another rainstorm. We don't say much to each other. We just sit there to keep one another company. I think back to the last rainstorm, when I gave Marc that advice on the dock, advice I wish I lived by. I can't believe he actually thinks I'm a good person. Then again, I haven't told him much about myself.

Ironically, right as I am thinking of him, Marc appears in our drive. "Hey, guys," he calls. He's been showing up a lot lately.

Matt greets him, and so do I.

"What's up?" I ask, looking up at him from the stairs.

"Well, Aly, I was wondering if you would like to go for a little walk with me. Sorry, Matt, I kind of wanted to talk to your sister in private."

"No problem, Marc." Matt smiles. "Not in the mood for walking anyway. I'd rather sit."

I look at Matt and then Marc. "Sure, I'll go," I reply standing up. "Matt, tell Grandma where I'm going."

"Will do."

"See you later!" Marc calls as we leave the driveway and walk onto the dirt road.

"So where are we going?" I ask.

Marc just smiles. "We are going to a special place of mine."

We continue down the road a ways until Marc stops and faces the forest. I see a little dirt trail winding its way through the maze of trees.

"The forest again?" I ask, looking at my almost healed scratches and remembering the last experience I had here.

"Oh, don't worry," Marc reassures. "We're walking on a trail this time. You won't get a single scrape."

"Well, if I do get scratched, I'm blaming it all on you," I joke as we enter the lush forest.

He silently guides me through the forest. When I'm not running for my life, the woodland is very pretty, calm, and peaceful. The canopy of trees protects us from the dark sky above, making me feel safe. We even see a deer bouncing through the forest. It hops along, feeling unnoticed. Its tan and white spotted head is held high. I stop and smile at the animal, thinking how rare a scene like this is in California.

The trail ends in a clearing protected by the flourishing aspens and oaks. Luscious green grass sprouts from the cleared land. Through all the dark clouds, a single ray of sun has managed to shine down in the middle of the clearing. I can see small particles of dust slowly floating in the light. A light breeze sways the delicate strands of dark green grass and the tree branches back and forth as if they are dancing.

"It's beautiful," I breathe.

"It is one of my favorite spots actually. I've been coming here ever since I was little. It's my secret place. In fact, the only other people I've brought here are Scott and Mr. Bennett, and that was years ago."

"Well, I'm honored that I get to experience such a beautiful place. This is something I rarely see in LA," I say, bending down to touch the petals of a single yellow flower. It feels shiny and soft to the touch.

"I have been thinking..." Marc says, looking down at me. I stand up in front of him.

"What have you been thinking?"

"This summer would have been very different if I hadn't met you..."

"Would it?" I laugh.

"Well, think about it. Think of all we've done. I feel like I have known you my whole life." He takes a step closer to me.

"Me too," I say, looking up at the dark clouds rolling in by the minute.

"It's going to be so different when you leave and we no longer get to see each other every day."

"I know," I say, trying not to picture having to go back to my real home. "But that's still far away."

He takes my hands. "But when it comes..."

"Don't say that," I reply, making him quiet. I look into his deep blue eyes, so filled with life, love, and compassion, and then I feel myself leaning toward him. He does too. Our lips almost touch, but then he says something.

"Aly, I really like you..." he whispers.

Then I know where this is going. The dinner. This walk. The way he is talking. I pull back. He looks at me, confused. "What are you doing, Marc?" I ask, beginning to wonder what I have gotten myself into. I knew this was bound to happen. I wanted it to, but I also refused to think that it could actually happen.

"I don't understand," he says.

"We're just friends...right? Remember what I told you. I didn't come here for this."

He looks at me and in a second, his eyes, once so full of life, look lonely. "Friends? Is that all you see me as?" he manages to say.

"What? Do you think I came all the way to Minnesota to fall in love? I could have easily done that in California."

I take another step back. He just stares at me, his face turning red, and I can tell he is suddenly extremely embarrassed.

"I came here to get my life together, not get distracted..." I say in a soft voice.

"I never had this plan in mind either... I just thought..." he chokes out.

"I'm sorry if I was leading you on, Marc, but I can't do this," I quietly say, "ever."

He looks hurt and his blue eyes seem shinier than they were

seconds before.

"You have to understand where I'm coming from. You're my friend. One of my best friends," I tell him, but he won't look me in the eye. He begins to walk back toward the trail.

"Marc," I call out.

"I think I understand now," he whispers. And then he runs. He runs as fast as he can out of the clearing.

"Marc!" I scream. "Marc! Don't go!" The single ray of sun has now disappeared, and I feel raindrops beginning to fall gently to the ground.

"I can explain!" I yell after him, but he continues to run.

And then a thought hits me, and I feel like I have just been punched in the stomach. Marc has never been in a relationship, and I suddenly know why. He has always feared rejection. That's why he looked so distraught. He has never tried to ask someone out before because he is afraid. I've just made Marc's biggest insecurity, biggest fear, and biggest nightmare come true right before his eyes. Rejection.

Then I know why he bolted out of the clearing so fast. "Marc!" I scream again. "Marc!" I get no reply. The rain is beginning to pick up now, and tears fill my eyes too, blinding my vision. I feel terrible, guilty. Why can't we just talk this out? I stumble onto the trail and begin to run as fast as I can, slashing through the underbrush. "Marc!" I yell again, but it's too late. He has already gone.

I make it back onto the main road. The rain is steady now and I'm drenched. I stand in the middle of the dirt road that is slowly becoming mud, and then I sink to my knees, weighed down with tears. I lie in the middle of the road bawling my eyes out. I cry for Marc, for my family, for the mistakes I have made. "Marc, please come back," I whimper, but he is nowhere in sight. I should have just let Marc kiss me.

I lie in the road, paralyzed by emotions, until Matt and my grandma find me. They must have seen Marc run by without me and decided to come looking. When they see me they help me to my feet. I want to say I can walk back myself, but I'm exhausted from all the crying, so I let them guide me back.

Once at the house, no one asks me what happened, which is good. But I think they know. I take a long, hot shower and curl up in my bedroom wearing sweats and a sweatshirt. I doze off for a while, but I later wake up, wide awake. I look at the clock, 8:37. It's getting close to night. I desperately try to fall back asleep, but with no luck. I decide to get up.

The upstairs floor is empty. Everyone must be on the porch or downstairs. Maybe I should join them. Then again, I'm not really in the mood. I walk down the narrow hall that connects my room and a neighboring room to the rest of the upstairs. The floor creaks under my weight. I run my finger down the smooth wooden wall and look up at the white ceiling above me. Then I stop and squint through my tired eyes. Above me I see the entrance to the attic.

I run back to my room and grab the desk chair. Back in the hall-way I stand on it and reach up, pulling down on the small door. It opens and I tug down on the ladder. I climb up into the dark space. The air is thick and warm, and I am forced to take off my sweatshirt. Blindly, I run my hand along the wall looking for a light switch. I finally find one and when I pull on it. the room glows golden.

The attic is old and unkempt. Wood boards cover the ceiling, walls, and floor. The walls arch up, forming a point in the middle. I am in the roof. I can only stand up straight in the center of the room. If I wish to venture any farther than the center I will have to bend down. A small window is positioned in the back of the room. When I look out I see the lake rippling away the raindrops.

Old cardboard boxes fill much of the space, along with other antique pieces of furniture covered with white sheets and various light fixtures. Curious, I begin to scan the titles of the boxes. Some are labeled *books, photo albums, kitchen wear*. I push those boxes aside, looking for something interesting. Then I see it. In the corner of the room, I see a medium-sized box labeled *CH Things*.

I half drag, half carry the box out of the corner and into the light. I take a deep breath. This is my mom's stuff. Cassidy Henderbell, now known as Cassidy Butler.

This is the stuff she had before she was a big model in Hollywood. I tear through the taped seal and pull back the cardboard flaps. I begin to carefully remove the items. Some books, various rocks from the lake, a teddy bear. Then I get to the pictures. I pull out a stack. I see my mom posing in photos with various friends at the lake. Like me, she and my grandparents would spend the summers here. They lived in New York, where my grandpa was an editor for a newspaper. She looks a lot like me. She has long brown hair and a similar smile. She wears simple denim shorts and a floppy T-shirt, stuff she wouldn't dare be caught in now. I smile, because the girl looking back at me reminds me of...well, me.

I see a picture of my grandparents, who look younger, and my mom posing in the living room in the cottage. They all look so happy. This must have been before my mom ditched them for a life of fame. I see pictures from my mom's first photo shoots. Then I notice a photo with three people sticking their tongues out. One is my mom, the other a girl, and the last one a guy. They look about my age. I flip to the next one and notice my mom with the same guy again. He has dark hair and familiar-looking eyes.

I set the pictures aside and continue to dig through the box. I find a journal. I flip through the pages, scanning for something interesting to read. Then I stop when I come across a familiar name. Maylore.

> *July 29*
> *Today I had to tell Sam goodbye. Not just for the summer, but forever. I love it here. He is staying, but I want to get my career going in LA. I don't have time for silly summer romances. Besides, I am sure there are plenty of great guys in California. He acted like he wasn't hurt, but I know he was. I told him we could still be friends, although I don't*

think he really cares. I feel bad, but what other choice do I have? LA will be great. I just need to forget this happened and move on. I should be excited because I am about to live my dream. I hope I am doing the right thing for both Sam Maylore and myself.

LA, here I come!

I look back at the picture. My mom knew Marc's dad. My mom knew Marc's dad. I let that sink in. Small world. They were friends, they liked each other, but they let thing get in the way and never spoke again. I hold up the picture of the two of them. The more I look at it, the closer the teenage boy resembles Marc. My mom did the same thing I just did to the boy down the street, though she never fixed it. She never made things right. I still have a chance. I know what I must do.

CHAPTER 12

The next morning, I wake up at seven and hurry to get dressed. I'm downstairs before Matt or even my grandma. I'm about to head out the door when my grandpa comes into the kitchen.

"Good morning, Alyson!" he calls, pouring himself a cup of coffee.

"Good morning," I reply, in a hurry to leave. "Can I borrow a bike?"

"Sure," he says, "but I think I have something you might like better. Follow me."

I follow him out of the house and into the garage.

"So where are you going?" he asks.

"To Marc's," I reply.

He walks over and begins to rummage through a drawer. I tap my foot impatiently. What could be a better source of transportation than a bike?

He turns around holding up a set of keys. Car keys. He tosses them to me. "I know the Maylores' isn't far, but I have been looking for an occasion to let you use the truck." He points to the old red truck in the last bay of the garage. "I know technically your parents said you are not allowed to have driving privileges, but you've gained our trust. You're ready."

I'm speechless. "Thank you!" I gasp, running to my grandpa and giving him a hug. "Thank you! Thank you! Thank you!"

I begin to walk toward the car.

"Alyson!" my grandpa calls after me. "You will need this!" He throws me my driver's license too. "I have had it locked in this drawer the whole time."

"Thanks!" I beam.

The inside of the red truck is old but comfortable. It's a stick shift, but that's what my dad taught me on when I was first learning to drive. One thing he actually did. I start it up and idle out of the garage down toward the Maylores'. It feels great to be back on the road.

I park in the Maylores' driveway. All their windows are propped open, allowing the morning breeze to seep into the home, so I know they're up. I casually walk up to the screen door and knock. Then I step back and wait. Seconds pass and Scott comes to the door.

"Hey, Aly!" he says, opening the door and inviting me into the spacious home.

"Is Marc around?" I ask.

Scott nods. "He's upstairs. Go on up."

"Thanks," I say, walking toward the wooden staircase. Scott seems pretty chill about letting me in, especially after what happened last night. I begin to wonder if Marc's family even knows what occurred between us.

When I get to the top of the stairs, I hear the faint noises of a guitar. The closer I get, the louder it gets, and I instantly know it is Marc. "Knock, knock," I quietly call, tapping on Marc's half-open door. I step in.

He looks up and the guitar falls silent. "What do you want?" he asks, looking slightly embarrassed.

"I came to talk to you..."

"There is nothing to talk about," he snaps back.

"Look, I know you don't want to talk to me, and this whole situation is incredibly awkward, but there is something I need to tell you, and I'm going to say it. When I'm done, if you still don't want to hear from me, we never have to talk again."

"Fine," he says, looking at the guitar strings.

Marc's room is painted gray with basketball posters on the wall. Everything is kept surprisingly clean and organized. I walk across the room and sit on a rolling chair pulled up to a wooden desk. "I kind of freaked out last night," I begin. He doesn't look at me. "I just never saw that coming. I thought we were more like friends, and I thought I made it pretty clear at the very beginning when I said that I didn't want to hang around you if you liked me more than that…"

"I know… The more I think about it, the more I see I was wrong," he whispers.

"Look, I know I was mean. I really like spending time with you, talking to you, getting to know you, and if we were ever in a relationship, that could all disappear. I care about you too much. Also, we live so far apart it would never work. You're a great guy, Marc. You just need to wait for the perfect girl, and when she comes you need to not be afraid to say how you really feel about her."

He looks up at me.

"The perfect person will come and when she does she will say yes. But for now I just want to be your friend." I pause. He doesn't say anything. "That's what I came to say." He still doesn't say anything. "That was the best apology I could come up with."

"I forgive you. I acted stupid too. I should have actually thought it through… I was just in the moment. I knew you didn't want to hear that." The room falls silent until Marc speaks again. "Aly, can I ask you something?"

"Yeah?"

"Tonight there is this party in town that some local teenagers are hosting. Nothing fancy, just a 'school' type party. I was wondering, if you weren't doing anything, maybe you would want to go with me? Not as a date of course…"

A party. I hesitate to reply.

"If you don't want to, that's totally cool. Eric and Chloe are going too, so I would have people to hang out with, but…"

I cut him off. "No, that would be fun," I say, forcing a smile.

"Good," he says, sounding relieved.

"Hey, we could all get ready at my house," I suggest.

"Get ready?" Marc looks at me. "How hard is it to get ready?"

"It's a girl thing." I laugh. "Okay, well, Chloe and I could get ready, and then you and Eric could meet us."

"Sounds good to me," he replies. "We want to go around nine."

"Nine..." I say. "That's kind of late..."

"Not really," he says, giving me a weird look. "If anything I would say it's early..."

"Well, are there chaperones?"

He looks at me. "Have you not been to a party before? It's a party, with high schoolers. Don't you want to have fun?"

"Yeah, I'm just kidding!" I force myself to laugh. The fear of having too much fun rushes through my mind.

"I've been trying to hear about or get invited to a party here for a while, and Chris and Andrew hooked Eric and me up. I can't wait!"

"It will be super fun!" I reply. "Well, I better get going. I have to get back home."

"All right, see you tonight then." He smiles, seeming back to his old self.

I begin to walk out the door, but then stop. "There's one more thing I came here to show you." I reach into my pocket and pull out the photo of our parents. I hand it to him.

"What's this?"

"That's my mom and your dad. I guess they knew each other when they were our age."

"They did?" He looks at the picture more closely. "They kind of look like us."

"I know," I reply. "Anyway, our parents decided not to talk to each other again. I couldn't have that happen after all we have been through."

He smiles. "Mind if I keep this for a while?"

"Not a problem." I smile, and I leave Marc looking at history that has seemed to repeat itself.

⸺◈⸺

Chloe comes over at seven to get ready. "So this event is pretty casual, right?" I ask. The two of us are sitting on the floor of my room deciding what to do first.

"Yes, but I think a lot of girls will be wearing skirts and dresses. It's a small-town thing. We like to dress up when we have the chance. Show off when we can, I mean. We dress so casually all the time here... The problem is, I still couldn't find anything; most of my good clothes are in Minneapolis."

I just smile at her.

"What?" she asks.

"Remember the first day I met you and you kind of made fun of me for wearing that outfit?"

"I did not make fun of you! But yes, I remember..."

"Well, I have two full suitcases of clothes like that. When I came, I totally brought the wrong stuff."

Her face lights up at the thought of new clothes. I pull open the curtain to my closet and drag out the two oversized bags that haven't been opened since Matt brought me my casual clothes from home. I unzip the bags. "Help yourself," I say.

We spend the next thirty minutes trying on clothes. It's weird, after wearing shorts and T-shirts for so long, to think that these were the kind of clothes I wore on a daily basis at home in LA. I find it fun though to look through stuff I haven't seen for so long. Chloe decides on a casual black dress with a cut-out back, and I decide on a deep blue skirt and a black crop top that lines up perfectly with the top of the skirt. We curl our hair, put on makeup, and complete the outfits with heels, though after about one minute of putting them on, we decide on sandals... They're too much. We look like LA girls going out to party. I smile at the thought of home.

"Marc and Eric will be here soon," Chloe says excitedly, preparing to go downstairs.

"Okay, I will be down in a second," I reply. When she leaves I look at myself in the mirror. I look just like the girl I left behind. I take a deep breath, trying to mentally prepare myself for the night ahead.

On my way out though, something catches my eye. Sitting in the pile of clothes that have been spread out on the ground, I see the small white cardboard box wrapped in a plastic bag. It hasn't even caught my attention until now, and I'm glad Chloe didn't notice it either. I throw it back into the suitcase, cover it with clothes, put the bag away, and head downstairs. I can't deal with looking at it right now.

Downstairs, Marc and Eric have already arrived. They are admiring Chloe's chic style. I walk into the room. I feel nervous, a feeling I rarely get. I have no reason to be.

When Marc sees me, he smiles. "Wow, Aly, you look great."

"Thank you."

"We need to get a picture of you all!" my grandma gushes, walking into the living room.

"This isn't prom," I tell her.

"I know, but I want a picture."

The four of us stand in the living room and smile. My grandma takes several pictures. I see Matt standing in the back of the kitchen, watching. "Hey, Matt!" I call. "Come take a picture with us."

He shakes his head. "Oh come on, Matt!" Chloe says.

"Come get a picture with us old people!" Eric jokes.

"Fine," Matt says. He joins our group. I put my arm around my little brother and smile.

"All right, Grandma," I say, after several more pictures, "we need to get going."

My friends leave the house, heading outside to the car. Matt looks at me with concern.

"Don't worry, Matt," I say, putting a smile on my face. "I'll be back soon."

"That's not what I am worried about."

"I'm not stupid," I reply. "It's just a party. I'm not going to do anything bad. I didn't even do anything bad last time."

"If you need us to come get you, we will," my grandma says.

"Please don't worry. It's just a small party in a small town. It will be fun."

For a small town, the party seems huge. Just from pulling up at the front, I can tell there are lots of people here. It's in someone's enormous vacation home. Music blares from the backyard, and I can see some sort of light system going. "This is a small-town party?" I ask Marc as he parks the car on the next block over. "This is bigger than some of the parties at home."

"Well, from the looks of things, there are more than just locals here. Let's go check it out!" Eric says. Chloe smiles with excitement.

We enter through the front door. The foyer is crowded with people entering the party.

"Let's go out back." Chloe pulls Eric through the crowd.

Marc and I slowly push through. In the living room, small groups of people talk and laugh in circles. "Do you want to go out back?" Marc asks. I nod and follow him into the backyard.

Outside, people dance in groups on the lawn. Some vague Indie song plays, and people are really getting into it. The lake is calm, and I notice some people have even pulled their boats up to the shore. I look across the lake to see if I can make out my grandparents' house, but it is too dark to tell where it is. I see Chloe and Eric on the dance floor, dancing with a group of people and laughing.

All around me people look like they are having fun, yet I can't seem to get into the mood. Maybe that is because my past is haunting me. The last time I went to a party, bad things happened after...

"So what do you want to do?" Marc asks, looking around in awe at the party scene.

I try to think of how to respond when I see Chris come up to Marc. "Hey, man!" He takes a drink of something out of a red plastic cup. "What's up?"

"Just got here," Marc replies. He seems completely fine talking to him today.

Chris laughs obnoxiously. "Of course you did. Who's the lady?" he asks, looking at me.

"Oh, this is my friend Aly. She lives down the street."

"Oh yeah, I remember you. We briefly met at the barbeque," he says, taking another drink from his cup.

I put a smile on my face and nod. "Hey, Marc," I say, trying to act casual, "I think I'm going to go find something to drink. I will be right back. You and Chris can catch up."

I turn toward the house before he can reply. I push my way inside. The place is more crowded than when we arrived just minutes before. I wonder whose house this is. Did their parents allow them to have this party, or did they decide to throw it while the adults were gone? Why am I having all these thoughts pop into my head? I've never had them before. I push those questions aside and walk toward the kitchen.

A teenager, about my age, with long, shaggy hair and hipster glasses calls out to me as I walk by. "Hey, you," he calls. "Care for a drink?"

"Sure." I smile, walking toward him. He must be in charge of drinks because as he calls to me, he adds several more red plastic cups to the sea on the counter. He picks one up and hands it to me. "Here you go." He grins.

I take the drink and look at it. A pink punch swirls in the cup. I take a sip. Definitely alcohol. Strong alcohol. I stumble back.

"Are you okay?" he asks me.

"I'm fine," I say, casually putting the cup back on the table. "If you will excuse me..."

I turn and walk away from the drink table as fast as I can. I knew this was a party-party. Just like the ones at home. I did know. I just didn't want to believe it because I didn't want to deal with it. I continue to push my way through the house, looking for a bathroom. The air seems heavy. My heart begins to pound. All the laughing and yelling is getting to me. I finally find one down an empty hallway. I rush in and lock the door. I'm finally alone.

My heart beats inside my chest, and I feel like I'm sweating. I put my hands on the edge of the sink and stare at my reflection in the mirror. I'm not ready to do this again. I just can't. It was a party that started my downfall. A stupid party, and I can't afford to do that again.

I want to stay with Marc and have a good time, but I know if I do, I will give into the thought that has been pounding in the back of my head for a month. I have no choice. I have to leave.

I try to calm myself. I splash water on my face to cool down. I stay locked in the bathroom until my breathing returns to normal. Then I unlock the door and leave the house as fast as I can.

<hr />

I will have to walk halfway around the lake to get home. I'm not thrilled, but I'm not about to disrupt my friends' fun and have them take me home. I take off my sandals, which for some reason are giving me blisters, and walk on the cold pavement of the sidewalk. The farther away I get, the fainter the music from the party becomes. In between the houses, I look out at the moonlit lake. The dark purple water lightens in the moon's path, showing its reflection. I hear a loon call out in the distance. The evening breeze brushes against my skin, cooling me down. Everything is so calm, so peaceful, unlike that party.

I swing my sandals in my hand and watch my bare feet step on the pavement. I prepare to turn the corner when I see a car driving slowly. It looks like it's following me. I take a deep breath. Do I run? No, that's stupid. I decide to act natural and pick up the pace. The car keeps creeping along behind me until it catches up with me. The driver rolls down the window. "Aly, what are you doing?" Marc asks from inside the car.

"Marc?" If only I'd looked more closely before, I would have recognized his Range Rover. "Marc, you scared me! I thought you were some creeper or something…"

"Nope, I'm definitely not a creeper." He laughs. "Why did you leave?"

I look at him, not knowing what to say. I don't want to lie to him anymore. I decide to avoid his question. "How did you know I left?"

"The guy serving drinks told me. He saw you leave. He said you kind of freaked out. So why did you leave?"

I take a deep breath. "I couldn't be in that sort of atmosphere," I quietly say, beginning to walk again. He slowly rolls the car along with me.

"So, what are you going to do, just walk back?"

I nod.

"Three miles in no shoes?"

"Do I have a choice?"

"Let me drive you home," he offers.

"No. You go enjoy the party. I know how excited you are."

"Eh, I will survive. Besides, who will I hang out with?"

"Some of the bazillion people inside," I reply.

"I'd rather hear about why you couldn't stand to be at a party. You seemed worried about it ever since I invited you..."

I stop walking. He stops the car. I look at him. I don't want to tell him anything, but I feel like I should.

"Here, I will make you a deal. I will give you a ride back, but I want to hear about your life story...why you really came here this summer."

So he knows. I don't hesitate. It's time I told him anyway. I nod and get in the car, leaving the party scene behind.

CHAPTER 13

I don't want to worry my grandparents by returning home early. My guess is they are expecting me out until at least eleven. Marc parks his car back at his house. His grandparents are visiting some friends for the weekend, and Scott is out.

We head around to the back of the house and walk down the hill to the dock. We both sit facing the lake. I set my shoes next to me and dangle my feet in the cool dark water. Marc takes off his shoes and does the same. It's weird to think that across the lake, Chloe and Eric are at that crazy party. Across the lake the music is blaring, people are dancing, laughing, having fun.

Marc doesn't say anything. He isn't one to push, but I know he is waiting to hear what I have to say. He is ready for his part of the deal. I take a deep breath and begin to speak.

"So if you haven't figured it out yet, I didn't exactly come here for vacation this summer..."

"I think I got that," he replies, still not looking at me. "I mean, from the moment you got here, you didn't seem like the 'lake girl' type. You didn't seem like you wanted to be here very much."

A slight smile forms on my face, though Marc can't see it in the dark. "My parents sent me to visit my grandparents for a month over the summer because they wanted me to get a grip on reality. I've kind of done some stupid things lately..."

"Did you get arrested?" Marc asks.

I look over at him. Surprisingly, his face looks serious.

I shake my head. "If I was arrested I wouldn't even be here..."

He nods slightly. "So what did you do?"

I can tell he wants me to get to the point.

"I lied…" I quietly say.

"You got sent halfway across the country because you lied?" he asks. I can't tell if he wants to laugh.

"No…well, yes… I lied a lot and really messed things up with my family."

"Please continue," he urges.

"Well," I put myself in the moment as if it were happening right before my eyes, "it all started after Carson Mitchell's party."

———◦(◦)◦———

I see myself standing in the foyer of my house. Everything is a slow spin and I desperately want to close my eyes and lie down. I see my parents yelling at me for sneaking out to go to some party they told me I couldn't go to. It was late, and my mom had just returned from some event. My dad, who had stayed home that night, realized I had snuck out my window, as usual. He locked it, forcing me to enter downstairs, where both my parents were waiting for me. After they were finished yelling about how reckless and immature I was, they grounded me. They took my cell phone, my car keys, my debit card, my computer, and my privilege to go out, other than for school. That was to last two weeks. They were sick of me partying all the time, getting drunk all the time, being reckless. There was nothing I could do to reason with them. I could only be mad.

I was mad because I had been caught and because my parents had all of a sudden "started caring." I had sneaked out to parties dozens of times before, and no one had ever noticed. Now, all of a sudden, they were concerned with what I was doing. Normally, they just did their own things.

I spent the first week of my grounding focusing on school and ignoring my parents, trying to seem angry with them. Things really were fine though, until I got a call from my friend Tiffany.

She called on Matt's cell phone. She had been my friend for years, so naturally she had my little brother's number. "Be quick," he said, bringing me the phone. "I have stuff to do. Plus Mom won't be happy if she sees you talking to one of your friends."

I thanked him and closed the door of my room.

"Hey, Tiffany!" I said, finally excited to talk to a friend outside of school.

"How's the grounding going?" she asked.

"It's fabulous..." I said. "Although that party was worth it."

"Yeah! It has definitely been the best one all year," she replied. "Plus you were crazy!"

I rolled my eyes. "Ugh, don't remind me. I hope you have a reason for calling me," I said, getting to the point. "I can't talk for long."

"Oh I do! Aly, the new line of Chanel wallets was just released. They are limited edition. Only one hundred of each design! And guess what? They have some at the Rodeo Drive location. They actually have them!"

"You're kidding!"

"Would I kid over something like that? We have been waiting for this line to come out for months! We need to go see them!"

"You know I can't get out of the house," I replied sadly.

"Can't you come up with an excuse?" she asked. "Go to the library or something?"

"Probably, but even then I don't have the money to get it. My parents took my debit card away. No more shopping for me."

"Just borrow one of their credit cards. That's what I'm doing to get one. Besides, my mom buys so much she won't even realize that a thousand dollars extra has been spent."

"They would notice..."

"Well, is there any way you could get money?"

I hesitated to reply.

I look from the dark eerie lake over to Marc. His blue eyes shine in the moonlight. He looks like he is listening contently.

"At that moment I remember thinking hard, but not about the consequences of stealing money to get a stupid designer wallet. I remember thinking about how I could get away with taking the money. How I could get away so that no one would ever know...and then I knew what I had to do."

"So what did you do?" he asks.

I smile bleakly.

<hr/>

"Aly? Aly?" Tiffany called through the phone. "Are you still there?"

"Tiffany," I replied, "pick me up at the library at 4:05 this evening. I know where to get the money."

When I hung up, I gave the phone back to Matt and went downstairs into the empty kitchen. My mom was at a meeting. My dad, who had a day off, had gone to the gym. Lily and Jake were out with the nanny, which left the house empty to Matt and me, and Matt was upstairs watching TV.

I sat at one of the bar stools for a while sipping a cup of water. I kept staring at the white door that led to the basement. Then finally I made up my mind: my parents wouldn't miss one thousand dollars. Especially when there were thousands of other dollars in the safe downstairs. They probably didn't even know how much was in there.

I quietly crept into the basement. My dad had given me the combination to the safe, just in case there was ever an emergency. It contained family papers, old jewelry, and naturally, lots of cash.

I held my breath as I keyed in the digits. I was sweating, breathing heavily, but I told myself I had no reason to be nervous. The door swung open. Without thinking, I quickly counted out the money and closed the door. My plan was in action.

My dad agreed to take me to the library when he returned from the gym. I told him I had a paper I had to work on and I needed *books, and access to a computer, since I was grounded from mine. My dad said I had one hour. Then he asked why I was so dressed up to go to the library. I looked down at my curly hair, heels, and sundress. I waved it off saying I always dressed like that, but in reality I just wanted to look good at the store. I climbed the steps to the library and pretended to enter the building. Not two minutes after my dad dropped me off, a shiny white car pulled up.*

⸺◦⟨◍⟩◦⸺

"Am I boring you?" I ask Marc.

He laughs out loud. "Boring me? No way, this is getting good. Keep going."

I continue.

⸺◦⟨◍⟩◦⸺

I picked out a shiny silver wallet. It wasn't an elaborate design, but it was chic and would go with just about anything. It was small and perfect for a couple of cards and an ID. I didn't have many wallets this size. I counted out the eleven hundred dollars (including the tax) and waited while the saleslady wrapped it up all fancy.

"Isn't this great!" Tiffany said as the saleslady handed her the bag with her blue wallet in it.

I smiled. "Now we can match!"

I was handed my bag. I thanked the saleslady and together Tiffany and I proudly strutted out of the designer store. We were two seventeen-year-old girls carrying bags containing pricy wallets.

⸺◦⟨◍⟩◦⸺

I look over at Marc again, still looking out over the lake. He still looks like he is listening. I'm glad he isn't saying anything...yet.

Walking out of the store felt great. I was excited to finally have the wallet, and I couldn't wait to take it to school and show it off. At home that night, no one said anything about the missing money. In fact, my parents were in such a great mood at dinner that they decided my grounding was up. They said they thought I had learned my lesson.

That was when the first wave of guilt went through me. Right after I had stolen the money from my parents, they decided to forgive me. I hoped then they would never find out what I did with the money.

The guilt wave didn't last long, and that night I found myself sitting in my closet fingering the wallet. I made up my mind to take it to school the next day.

But that morning as I was getting ready for school, I heard my parents yelling. And when I went down for breakfast, my dad came rushing into the kitchen. Our housekeeper offered him coffee, but he said he was busy. Then he looked over at Matt and me, who were sitting at the counter. "Did either of you open the safe recently?" he asked, tying his tie. My stomach dropped.

"No," Matt replied through a bite of pancake.

I shook my head, trying to put a concerned look on my face. "No, is everything okay?" I asked.

"Oh yeah, I was just wondering if you two still knew the combination."

"Yeah, I do," Matt said, "but I have no reason to open it."

"Yeah, I know," he said. "You two have a good day at school." Then he left the kitchen. When he got back upstairs I could hear him yelling at my mom again. They knew the money was gone.

In my room I hid the wallet, and the bag, and the receipt. I planned to take it back after school and replace the money before things got out of control.

But after school when I saw the wallet again, I didn't want to take it back. It was so pretty, not to mention it was designer. I decided to hide it and wait for it all to blow over. In a couple of weeks, my parents would forget the money was missing. They hardly ever looked in the safe anyway. What were the odds they checked today? I stuffed the wallet between some warm winter sweaters in a high cabinet.

After two weeks of tension over me sneaking out, my relationship with my parents had returned to normal. I had always had a very distant connection with them, but that was what I had always known. I started sneaking out on the weekends again. No one noticed. I guess they thought I had learned my lesson.

I came home one day from school, earbuds in my ears blaring music and phone in hand texting, to find my parents both standing in the foyer. I closed the door, set my schoolbooks down on the ground, pulled my earbuds out, and smiled.

They didn't smile back. My dad began to talk. "Do you remember three weeks ago when I asked you if you had recently been in the safe?"

I casually nodded.

"You didn't take any money from there, did you? Maybe...let's say, over one thousand dollars?"

My stomach knotted and I felt my heart begin to race. I suddenly knew where this was going.

"No, I thought I told you that already..." I said, reaching down to pick up my books. I turned toward the stairs.

"Not so fast..." my mom said.

I turned back around. "Then what was this Chanel wallet with a receipt for almost that much doing in your room?" she asked. "It was hiding up in your sweaters. I found it there while looking for one of my shirts."

"Um...well..." I stuttered. "I bought it with my debit card, remember?" I hoped that would stop them from asking any more questions.

"Really, because the date on the receipt is the day before the *money went missing. And as your father recalled, it was the same day you were grounded, and the same time he had taken you to the library... Can you explain that?" She was raising her voice. I didn't realize they paid such close attention.*

I opened my mouth to say something, but nothing came out. There was nothing left to say. They had caught me red-handed.

"I didn't think so," my mom said in a soft, disappointed voice.

———◦《◦》◦———

"So that's what I did to get myself sent here. I, one, partied all the time and, two, stole money from my parents to get a stupid wallet," I quietly say, not making eye contact with Marc.

He doesn't say anything.

"Honestly, I never even really wanted that wallet. There were dozens of other things I could have bought that I wanted way more. It would be stupid for me to have a wallet of that much value. I think I did it because I was mad at my parents for grounding me for sneaking out. It was my way of showing them that I could get away with what I wanted. For years they hadn't cared about or noticed what I did. Then one day they just decide to ground me after I had been getting away with it for so long. I wanted to show them that they were oblivious to my actions.

"So, when they told me about this trip, and told me I was going because I had to experience 'real life,' a life where people don't steal one thousand dollars, let alone have one thousand dollars to get a wallet, I told them it was their fault that I did what I did. I also told them they were cowards and that this was their way to get rid of me. I said a lot of bad stuff that night, stuff I don't think they will ever forgive me for. The thing is, it was one hundred percent my fault, and I see that now.

"So maybe that wasn't the story you were looking for. Maybe you were waiting to hear me say I was arrested or crashed a car or had a problem with drugs and alcohol, but I realized I had a conscience. A conscience that knew right from wrong, and that is why I have felt so haunted recently, because I knew what I did wrong. I knew I messed up.

"Being here has brought me back to reality, but also it has shown me the importance of relationships. At home, though sad to admit, I think I cared more about what I had, what I did, and what I could get more of than who I was with. The first day I got here, Chloe asked me why I was so dressed up. When I looked down at myself, I saw designer labels and limited editions, but not a girl that was just 'dressed up.' That evening I stood in front of the mirror in a simple shirt and shorts and just looked at myself. And all I saw was a girl. I was no longer the girl with the designer clothes, the nice car or big home. I was just a girl. I didn't even know who I was. I didn't know if I was nice or caring or funny..." I pause. "I had spent so long with the material side of life, I hadn't bothered to develop true relationships...and that was when I decided I had to stay here. I had to accept the facts. I had to change my life, because it seemed pretty crappy right then. And look what has happened: I became close to my grandparents. My brother. I met Chloe and Eric and Mr. Bennett, and I met you, Marc. You were the one willing to give me a chance when no one else would.

"I made some pretty bad mistakes this year, and I regret them all, but if I had never come here, never partied hard or stolen money, I would still be in LA, living the conceited, materialistic life I had, and I would never have learned who I really could be."

I sigh, thinking back to the day my parents caught me, and then I look at Marc. He is looking at me, expressionless. I keep talking.

"That is why I don't want to go home. I never meant to be a 'bad kid,' as my parents would say. I was just lost, angry, and in need of attention. I messed up bad, but that isn't the kind of person I am. I never wanted to hurt so many people in my life, especially my family. I have a conscience, unlike a lot of people I know. I know stealing is wrong. I know I shouldn't lie. That conscience makes me feel guilty all the time for what I did. I want to be the girl that you know, that my grandparents and Eric and Chloe know. Not the girl who everyone in LA knows..."

Marc smiles at my conclusion. "Then be that girl. I mean, why spend your life hiding behind some fake person? People change, they make mistakes, and they grow up. When you get home show them that you have grown up and changed for the better. Show them who you really are, and who you have always been."

"Thank you, Marc," I reply, staring out at the dark water lapping on the shore. "I'm sorry I took you from the party. It just brought me back to a bad place."

"I'm glad I finally got to hear about the real you," he replies. He extends his hand. I look at him, those blue eyes shining in the moonlight. I take his hand. He shakes it. "Alyson Butler, it's a pleasure to finally meet you."

✦

Marc drops me off at my house a little later. I'm early, but tired. This is the latest I have been out by myself in a long time. I smile, thinking it feels great to be trusted again.

I'm glad I finally told Marc. Glad I don't have to lie anymore. Everything is out in the open, and that is the way things are supposed to be.

I slowly walk into the dark house and take my sandals off so I don't make any noise. I begin to tiptoe toward the steps. The whole house is dark, except for the light of the moon that reflects in the large glass doors.

"You're back," I hear as I climb the first step.

I turn around. "Matt, what are you doing up?"

He is sitting on the couch and turns around to face me. "Couldn't sleep." He shrugs. "So how was the party? I thought you would be out later."

"Well, I was only there for five minutes. It was quite the scene though. I didn't know there were so many crazy teenagers around here."

"So you didn't stay?"

"No, it made me think too much of home...so Marc and I left. I told him why I came here this summer."

"And what did he say?"

"Not much, but he seemed okay with it. You know, it feels so good to have everything out in the open. I don't have to lie and pretend with him anymore." I smile and look at Matt. "I'm off to get some sleep," I say, turning toward the steps. "Hope you can fall asleep soon." I begin to climb the stairs.

"Aly, wait!" Matt calls back at me. I look back at my younger brother.

"I was down here because I was thinking..."

"Good to know..." I say, not quite sure how to reply. "Is there something you want to talk about?"

He nods. "Does it really feel that good to just say what you have to say even if you are afraid the other person might think of you differently?"

"Matt, what's going on?" I ask in a soft voice.

"If I tell, do you promise you won't be mad at me?"

"How could I be mad at you, Matt?" I look into my brother's concerned eyes.

He takes a deep breath. "Do you remember the night before you got grounded, and you went to Carson Mitchell's party?"

"How could I forget?" I sigh.

"Well, you snuck out your window, and when you came back it was locked, right?"

I slowly nod, not sure where this is going.

"It was me."

I look at him, confused.

"I'm the one who told Dad you had snuck out. I'm the one who told him you weren't home..."

"Why would you do that?" I ask, feeling a little betrayed.

"You don't know this, but I heard you sneak out every time. I would hear the window slide open from my room next door. You did it so frequently that I began to keep a tally. I didn't want to say anything, because it was your secret and your decision…"

"Then why did you tell?" I ask, cutting him off.

"Because I had to! Aly, you are my older sister, my role model. I know what you would do when you would sneak out. I heard about Chase Smith, Gabby Shell, and Logan Tadeligh's parties. Do you have any idea how hard it is to hear you come back at two in the morning, and then see you for breakfast and pretend like nothing happened? Aly, you came back totally wasted sometimes. Do you know how hard it was to see you, the person I saw as my kind, caring, innocent sister the next day and pretend like you weren't hungover? I heard stories about you from other kids at school. I was scared for you every time you left the house. Scared you wouldn't come back the same. It got to a point where I couldn't listen to you go out to those parties anymore, I couldn't think of you becoming one of those 'careless, crazy, party kids' I hear about at school all the time. So I told Dad, and made him promise that you would never know it was me who tipped him off.

"I'm sorry, Aly. If it weren't for me you wouldn't be here. If it weren't for me you would have never been grounded and you would have never stolen the money. That is why I had to come out here. I had to experience your summer trip because I played a role in it. You can't be mad at Mom and Dad for suddenly caring and being nosy because I was the one who told them. I was the one who made them aware. If I hadn't said anything, I bet they wouldn't even know… I didn't want to tell you…ever. But the guilt keeps building inside of me. I feel responsible for getting you in so much trouble with them." His voice cracks and he falls silent, tears beginning to well in his eyes.

At that moment I want to be angry with him. I want to yell at him for, as I would have said a month ago, "ruining my summer." But I just can't. Not when I see my brother, normally so composed, so mature, nearly in tears.

"It's okay," I whisper, looking into his eyes.

"It's what?" he whimpers. I don't think he believes the words I have just said.

"Why should I be mad at you for caring? Why should I yell at you for wanting to help me?" I choose my words carefully. "Matt, without you I would still be going to those parties. I wouldn't have a care in the world. I would only care about myself and what I had and what I did. I was lost, and if you hadn't brought me back to reality, I would still be looking for a way to do something I probably shouldn't be doing." I pause and begin to quietly laugh.

"What?" he asks me.

"If this was a month ago, I probably would have ripped your eyes out..."

A slight smile forms on his serious face.

"But it isn't. I'm so glad I came here this summer. Thank you for finally telling me."

"So you're not mad?"

I shake my head and sigh. A look of relief crosses his face.

"I just want to get this whole thing past us. I just want to forget all the crap I did. Forget all the lying and stealing and sneaking out and have a fresh start. This whole summer I have been clinging to it because I was afraid to let it go. But I think I am ready now, and to prove it to myself, there is something I have to do. Will you help me?"

I exit the house carrying a plastic bag under my arm. Though it's still dark I can still see perfectly, for there is not a cloud in the sky and the moonlight radiates across the lake.

Matt is at the shore, dragging one of the long canoes into the water. I have changed into shorts and a sweatshirt and when I reach the shore, I help him launch it. We both slip in and grab a paddle. Together we begin to row into the light pathway the moon makes for us. We row in silence, for the night is calm and I don't think either of us wants to disturb it. The crickets' chirping fades as we get farther and farther from shore. I hear a loon call in the distance.

Then the lake is filled with silence again until another calls back. The lake is calm. The only exception is when our paddles penetrate the surface, creating a pool of ripples.

The water grows darker the farther out we get, until we hit black water below us.

"Is this deep enough?" Matt asks me.

"Yes," I quietly reply, looking at the darkness around us.

"Well, what are we doing out here?"

"We have to get rid of this," I say, pulling out the plastic bag from beneath my legs.

"What's 'this'?"

I open the bag and pull out a white cardboard box. Carefully, I set it on one of the benches. I stare at it for a minute before opening the lid. I reach inside and pull out an object wrapped in white tissue paper. I undo the tape, and the tissue paper falls to the bottom of the canoe, revealing a shiny silver wallet.

"Aly, why do you have that?" Matt asks, wide-eyed.

——⟫«(◉)»⟪——

My mom comes into my closet. "How's the packing going?" she asks. I shrug, not wanting to talk to her.

"You might want to bring some casual clothes," she suggests as she watches me put a silk shirt into my suitcase. "It's just a small lake town."

I still don't respond and make an effort to put an even more extravagant top in the bag.

"Alyson, you know this is what is best for you..."

"Best for me? Or best for you?" I snap.

"Fine, if you are going to be rude, I'll just get to the point of why I came in here."

I continue to pack in silence.

She hands me the wallet. "Your father and I think it would be best if you hold onto this for a while. Find some use for it, since it cost us a small fortune."

I shake my head. "I don't want it," I say harshly.

"Then why did you spend our money on it?"

"Can't you just take it back?" I ask, almost pleading. "I just want to forget!"

"That's the thing, Alyson, we don't want you to forget. You betrayed us. You took advantage of us, your family. And we don't want you to forget what you did. Not yet anyway."

I look at my mom in disgust. "Fine, let me take the wallet that ruined my life, and take your great parenting advice and look at it every day!" I pick up a white cardboard box lying on the floor, wrap the wallet in tissue paper, tape it, and shove it in.

"Happy?" I ask, my eyes narrow and my voice unforgiving.

"I'm done with your attitude, Alyson! Be ready to go tomorrow morning," and with that she leaves the room.

I thrust the box into the depths of my suitcase and sink to the ground crying.

I haven't looked in that box until tonight.

"Mom thought it would be a good idea that I don't forget, but I have learned my lesson. I accept that I made mistakes, and I'm ready to let go. I need to move on." Tears begin to form in my eyes.

Matt doesn't protest. He doesn't say anything, but the look on his face says he agrees with what I am about to do.

I take one more look at the shiny leather, the fancy clasp, and the designer name etched in with a fine tool. I quickly remember the feeling I had when I first bought it. The feeling I got when I pictured myself using it, pulling it out in front of people. That feeling of excitement has faded. It makes me feel sick. I'm sorry, I think. I am ready to forget.

And with that I throw the wallet out of the boat. I throw it as far as I can. It hits the dark lake with a splash, sending ripples in all directions. I stand up to watch it vanish into the depths below. Then it's gone, and the water becomes calm again. I sit back down and look over at Matt. He gives me a slight nod.

We are silent on the trip back, but I feel different. I feel like the guilt and the pressure have lifted. I am ready to be the person I want to be. The person I think I am supposed to be.

———— ◍ ————

After I've told him everything, Marc treats me exactly the same. I'm not sure why, though. I think I would be slightly afraid if the person I had been hanging out with all summer had some, well, issues. Still Marc doesn't seem bothered.

Several days after the party, Marc and I go to Mr. Bennett's. As usual we sit on his porch, just talking. Marc lies out on his back, looking up at the ceiling while he and Mr. Bennett discuss this season's fishing tournament. I stand in the corner looking at a shelf of Mr. Bennett's items. It's odd to hear them talk to each other. It's almost as if they are father and son. They seem to know each other so well.

I turn my attention away from the conversation and back to the shelf. I see a small leather-bound book in between a stack of novels. It stands out to me because it is the only one without a title on the spine. I pull it out and flip it open. On the fraying pages I see old photos hand-taped into the book. I see a picture of a young Mr. Bennett and a woman. I see the woman again in several different pictures. In addition, there are pictures of various homes and activities, like fishing. "What's this?" I ask when the conversation pauses.

"Ah," Mr. Bennett sighs happily, "that is my book of everything that is special to me. Photos of my wife, my house, me fishing and biking, basically everything and everyone who has played an important part in my life."

"That's so special." I smile, preparing to place the book back on the shelf.

"Actually, Alyson, if you don't mind I would like to take a look at it. It has been a while, after all." He slowly readjusts himself in his chair and sighs.

I bring him the book, and he flips through the pages. "Look," he says, smiling at a memory. He turns the book toward us. "This is when my wife and I first moved into this house. She only got to live here five years..." he says with a sad face.

"What happened to her?" I ask gently.

"Heart attack," Mr. Bennett replies. "That would have happened twenty years ago next week. We were only sixty-five when she passed away."

"I'm so sorry," I whisper.

"It was hard, but I cherished every moment I had with her. You know, kids, you need to appreciate everyone in your life because you never know when someone can disappear."

I nod, thinking of my family.

Marc and I have now switched places. I have slumped down on the ground to listen intently, and Marc is standing up to look at the shelf I have just been looking at. "Look!" he suddenly says, sounding excited. "It's a Polaroid camera!"

"Polaroid camera?" I ask.

"Yeah, you know, the kind that shoots the pictures out the front when you take them."

"Oh yeah," I reply.

"Does it work?" he asks Mr. Bennett.

"Try it." The old man smiles.

"Smile, Aly!" Marc approaches me like a paparazzi. I turn and smile at the camera, pretending to be a model. Then I burst out laughing. The picture rolls out the front of the camera. Marc pulls it out, shaking it in the air until the image becomes visible. "Very nice," he says.

"You're like a professional photographer." I laugh, taking the camera from him. "Now it's your turn."

He smiles. When the picture comes out, I hand it to him. "Not bad," I say. "Hey, let's get one with Mr. Bennett!"

Marc and I get on either side of Mr. Bennett's armchair. "Make a face," Marc says at the last minute." I hold the camera out as far as I can, aim it back at the three of us, and snap the picture.

It comes out. "Perfect!" I say. In the picture Marc makes some weird face, Mr. Bennett sticks his tongue out, and I blow a kiss.

"Can I keep the pictures?" Mr. Bennett asks.

"Of course!" I say, handing him the three images.

We spend the rest of the afternoon at Mr. Bennett's, talking and laughing about life.

<hr />

Chloe is heading back to Minneapolis for a week to see her parents, so we decide to spend our last day together for a while playing a two-on-two game of basketball with Marc and Eric. My brother refs. Even though I can't really shoot a basket to save my life, I play anyway. I'm on a team with Marc, and Chloe and Eric team up.

Marc and Eric are really good and carry the competitive side of the game. As for Chloe and me, when we are actually lucky enough to get to shoot, or try, everyone stands back, giving us the benefit of the doubt. Marc and I win, and I'm surprised since I missed nearly every shot I attempted. I guess Marc pulled more than his weight. Eric and Chloe congratulate us. Eric isn't even mad or jealous.

The five of us then go down to the swing in Marc's yard where I first hung out with everyone. It's weird to be back here. More than a month ago, I stood here wanting so desperately to go home. Now I'm dreading my final days here. We all sit in the grass looking out over the lake. Everything here is perfect.

CHAPTER 14

That night I dream I'm running through the forest behind the house, looking for Marc. I scream his name, yet he never replies. The forest is darker than usual, and dried branches that crawl across the ground in unusual patterns have replaced the lush bushes. The sky is gloomy, but not like the night. It is literally black, as if no world exists at all. I continue to run. Then I see him, shriveled up against a tree. I try to run to him, but then I hear a slam...

I jolt up in bed and look at the clock, 3:00 a.m. Some noise just woke me up. I wonder if my grandparents are up, or Matt. Maybe one of them went to get some water. I peek out into the hall. Everyone's doors are closed. That's weird, I think. I climb back in bed. It must be my imagination playing tricks on me. I begin to drift back into a deep sleep when I hear another slam. This time I sit up wide awake and alert. Someone is definitely up, but not in my house. The noise came from outside. I peer out my open window that looks toward Chloe's house. That's where the noise came from. Then another thought hits me. Chloe and her grandparents are in Minneapolis. The house is empty, or should be.

My stomach drops. The robbers. That is the only reasonable answer. But what am I to do? Call the cops? They will be long gone by the time anyone arrives. I have no choice but to protect my friend's belongings myself. At least that's the first thought that pops into my mind. I quickly change out of my pajamas and throw on the first pieces of clothing I see, a denim button-up blouse and some black soft shorts. Then I creep down the stairs.

In the living room I look out the window to see if I can see anything going on at my neighbors', but the dense trees block my view.

I quietly unlock the door, but before I go I grab the home phone and dial 911. Then I set it down and let it ring. Even if I don't answer, they will come looking to see what is going on. I slip out of the house unseen and unnoticed.

As I creep across the lawn, the reality of what I'm doing sets in. I am no hero. I have no weapon to protect myself. These could be the robbers, and they probably know how to get someone out of their way. Nevertheless, I have to try. I have to try for Chloe's sake, for the neighborhood's sake.

I sneak through the underbrush and then stop when I'm in view of Chloe's drive. Everything looks normal, quiet. The door looks closed and locked. The windows are not broken. There looks to be no one in sight. I sit back on my heels, wondering if I really did hear a door slam. Was it just my imagination? Am I paranoid?

Great, I have just called the cops, and they'll be here soon. With nothing going on, I'm going to have to come up with a good story as to why I bothered them in the middle of the night. I wait for several more minutes, nothing. Feeling disheartened, I prepare to go back and face my punishment for calling the police. Chloe's house is fine. I stand up and take a couple of steps forward, but then I throw myself to the ground when I hear a noise.

I peer back through the bushes toward the house. It looks fine, but then I hear voices. I look across from the wooden home to see two figures wearing black emerging from the garage.

"Who would have ever thought that someone keeps a safe under their garage?" One of the figures laughs. His voice sounds familiar.

"Well, if you would have never done that gardening work for Coleman last year, you would have never known," the other replies.

"That was one worthwhile job," the first one says. "Now let's go check the house and get out of here!"

The two begin to walk toward the wooden porch on the front of Chloe's house. Halfway across the yard one sticks his hand out, signaling for the other to stop. "Did you hear that?" he says, sounding nervous.

"No, Andrew, shut up! You're psyching yourself out," the other replies, and I now recognize the voice as Chris'.

Andrew and Chris have been behind this whole thing. I should have known. They were the only ones who weren't at the barbeque...the one they were invited to during the time of the robbery. Everyone wrote them off as possible suspects because they were the ones who "discovered" the first robbery. In a sense they turned themselves in. It was all part of their plan.

"There it is again," Andrew whispers as Chris begins to move back toward the house.

"I heard it this time; someone is here..."

I cringe, hoping they haven't heard me. I hold my breath and try not to move as the two check the perimeter of the house. I see Andrew approaching me. The moment he looks over the bush I'm hiding behind, he will see me. I'm a goner. I squeeze my eyes tight just waiting for it all to be over. His footsteps get closer, then suddenly stop right in front of my bush.

"Andrew," I hear Chris say in a low voice, "got him!"

Andrew's footsteps begin to fade away. Him? Confused, I open my eyes and peek through the shrubbery, and then my heart feels as if it stops. Together the two of them pull Marc from the bushes on the other side of the house. He collapses on the ground in front of them.

"Couldn't stay away from us?" Chris laughs.

"Let go of me," Marc hisses, sitting up.

"Oh, shut up, Marc," Andrew says, a sick grin on his face. "So you figured out our little plan?"

"I was going to tell soon enough. I can't bear to keep your secret," Marc says between clenched teeth.

"So, you're going to tell on us? I wouldn't do that if I were you..." Chris taunts.

"What are you going to do to me if I waltz down to the police station and tell them right this second?" Marc retorts. His deep blue eyes catch the glimmer of the moon.

"Well, for one thing I will start with this." Chris kicks Marc in the stomach, sending him back to the ground. Marc, having not seen that coming, rolls over in pain and glares at the two figures above him. "And then if you dare tell a soul, I will just make the pain worse."

"Oh, so you're going to beat me up? Blackmail me? Ruin my life?" Marc laughs, trying to stay calm, although I can tell he is becoming nervous. "Because that isn't obvious at all."

"I will do it," Chris states, stepping just inches from where Marc lies on the ground. "I will do it now." He pulls a pocketknife from his pocket and flips the blade out, aiming it at Marc. He looks nervous.

Marc becomes silent. He tries to sit up, but Andrew kicks him down again, sending him groaning in pain. "You better shut up, Maylore," he says.

I have to act now. I know Marc can't fend for himself forever.

"You won't do anything," I say, standing up from behind the bush, instantly blowing my cover.

"Aly?" Chris says, unsure what to do. He aims his incredibly small knife from me to Marc several times before deciding to continue to hold it toward Marc.

"Aly?" Marc says, confused. "Get out of here!"

I don't listen to him. "You won't do anything. You can't," I calmly say, approaching the group.

"Oh, yes, I can," Chris shoots back, trying to sound mean.

"Really?" I say, beginning to pace back and forth. "For starters, why are your hands quivering so much?"

Chris looks down at his hands and tries to keep them steady, but it doesn't work.

"See what I mean... You don't want to hurt anyone. You wouldn't even have to, but the pressure of what you are doing is getting to you. You're no thief...you're just some teenage boy caught up in the wrong game."

"Stop moving!" Chris says, pointing his knife toward me.

"Aly, watch out!" Marc yells, but Andrew rushes to his side and covers his mouth with a sweatshirt.

I stop and put my hands up in the air in a surrendering motion.

"I don't want to cause any harm," I say, looking Chris directly in the eye. "Besides, how much damage can that little knife really do?"

"Then why are you still here?"

"Doesn't matter," I reply. "What does matter is that we make a deal."

"What kind of deal?" Chris asks, keeping the knife toward me.

"You put that knife down and let Marc and me go, and we won't tell anyone. Then you and Andrew can continue to go freely about your robbing sprees unnoticed."

Marc's eyes show true terror as I say this.

"How can I trust you?" Chris asks.

"I know where the house key to Chloe's house is. I want to help."

"You do?" Chris says.

I nod and take several cautious steps toward the wooden house. Then near a bush, from under a rock I pull out the spare key. Chloe needed it once when we came home from Marc's.

"Not so fast..." Chris says.

I stop. Marc yells at me through the cloth. I can't make out what he is saying, but I know he wants me to stop.

"How can I trust you?" Chris asks again suspiciously.

"I know how you feel, and I don't want you to get caught," I state. "Once you're caught, it's all over."

"What are you talking about?" Andrew asks, making sure Marc is on the ground.

"Well, I stole a lot of money from my parents, and unfortunately they found out. I was in your shoes and if there would have been that person to help me, to be my ally, I would have succeeded. You have to believe me... Besides, what harm is done with making a little money on the side? It's like a summer job, but you hardly have to work."

"Aly, don't do this!" Marc yells through the sweatshirt. Andrew pushes it in harder, forcing Marc to gag.

"What about him?" Chris asks, looking back at Marc lying on the ground.

"Oh, he will listen. He will listen to me, especially because if he doesn't, we can blame him for these robberies." I glare at Marc.

He looks at me. "You realize if you are lying to me and you tell about what we are doing, we will make your life miserable."

I swallow and reluctantly nod, wondering what Chris means.

A smile slowly spreads across Chris's face; then it fades. He is deeply contemplating my offer.

"Now, how about you give the knife to me," I say, still trying to stay calm, although the inside of my body is shaking with all the pressure.

"You don't seem like the stealing type or the type of person who would let your best friend take the blame for your actions. But I can see a side of you, a side of you that wants to rebel, a side that is looking for mysterious attention."

"You do?" I gulp, looking at Marc's petrified eyes. He can't believe what I'm saying, what I'm doing, who I'm becoming.

Chris looks at Andrew, who gives a slight nod. Chris takes a deep breath and then flips the knife away and slides it to me. I pick it up and toss him the key. He catches it. It is then that I hear police sirens in the distance.

Thinking quickly I turn around and break into a run toward Andrew, while flipping the knife back out. Andrew, being the coward that he is, releases Marc. He freezes, staring directly at me. Marc then jumps up and tackles Chris. He pins him down on the ground. I quickly make my way toward Andrew and grab the back of his arms.

"You called the cops, didn't you?" Chris hisses.

I nod. "Just taking precautions. Oh, and also, next time you want to break into a house, try being quieter. I could hear you from my room next door."

"You tricked us..." Chris whines.

"You tricked the whole neighborhood, telling them someone had broken into a house when you did it all along..." I reply, right as the cops pull into the drive.

Several policemen exit the car and run to take Chris and Andrew from our grip.

"These are your robbers," I say to one of the policemen, tossing him the bag of stolen goods from the safe that lie in a heap with Andrew's sweatshirt.

He opens the bag and looks through the contents. "Did you breach a personal safe?" he asks Chris and Andrew.

Chris just glares. Andrew nods, looking perplexed.

"Are these the only people we are arresting?" His gazes takes in all four of us.

I look at Marc, who looks back at me.

"Yes," Andrew replies. "It was just the two of us. They had no clue what we were doing. They were in the wrong place at the wrong time."

The officers handcuff the two boys and begin to haul them to the cars. One of the policemen looks at Marc and me. "You again," he says. "How come every time there is a robbery at night, you two seem to show up?" He chuckles to himself.

I shrug. Marc doesn't say anything.

By now people are beginning to emerge from their homes. I see my grandparents come outside, followed by Matt and some other neighbors.

I turn to go but Marc grabs my arm.

"Thank you," he says, looking into my eyes. "I don't know what I would have done without you back there." He looks back to where Andrew pinned him. "You're a good actress."

I shake my head. "You knew this whole time? You knew what Andrew and Chris were up to, but you didn't tell anyone?"

"Aly, no I didn't, let me explain..."

But I don't let him finish. "You lied to me."

"No, you don't understand. Please, let me explain," he replies.

"How did you know Chris and Andrew were here? How did you know they were the robbers? How did you know their plan, Marc?"

"Well... you see..." he stutters, trying to form words.

"Please talk to me, Marc," I say, suddenly fearing the guy I have begun to call my best friend is a flat-out liar.

"I was at my house and..."

"And what?" I cut him off, needing a response. But I'm afraid of what he might say. Afraid of what he knows. I can't let him finish. I just can't. "Marc...don't tell me you're a liar..."

"I'm not. My choices were limited..."

I cut him off again. "We always have a choice, the choice between right or wrong."

"Well, look who's the one to speak," he replies, suddenly drawing the subject toward me. "You have been making the wrong decisions for years, and you never really cared. You just cared about yourself. You just wanted attention. You can't call me a liar when we all know you have been lying to people for years, even the people who really cared about you."

"Don't you dare say that!" I reply, raising my voice. Marc's comment stings, making tears well in my eyes. "These are two completely different things and you know it!" and then I pull away from him, but I turn back for one last thing. "You think you know me so well..." I shake my head. I can't talk to Marc right now. I can't sort things out, not after what he has just said.

"As do you," he retorts. "You don't know for a second how hard my life has been. You're not the only one with problems, Aly! It isn't all about you!"

Then he turns and leaves me raging in fury in the middle of Chloe's yard. I watch him go for a split second, then I turn toward my family.

I don't know what just happened between Marc Maylore and me, but I hope that's the last conversation we ever have.

CHAPTER 15

I get in trouble for sneaking out in the middle of the night, even if I was only next door tricking the robbers. I'm not punished though. My grandparents just talk to me about trying to make better decisions, decisions that are safe and worthwhile.

I'm done trying to make things right with Marc. In fact, the next morning I try to pretend that I never even knew him. It doesn't work so well. What if he really did lie to me? I spent all summer trying to trust people again, and I trusted him, only he was a liar. But I don't want to know. I don't want to go talk to him. What he said to me hurt, and I didn't think words like that would ever come from him. I'm too mad to sort things out this time. I need a break. Maybe if I distance myself, I will be ready to go ask Marc for the truth.

My grandma lets me sleep in, and I roll downstairs around nine. She tells me I have to go to the police station at noon to give a statement about last night. I make myself breakfast and eat it quietly at the table. "I'm going to Mr. Bennett's in a few minutes to drop off some groceries. Would you like to come with me?" my grandma asks, trying to cheer me up. I think she knows something happened last night with Marc.

"Sure," I say, shoveling cereal into my mouth. "Mr. Bennett's is always fun." I quickly finish and we load the car and go.

A thick layer of fog covers the lake today. In fact it is so thick I can't even see the shoreline from the road. The sky is cloudy and there's mist in the air, though it is not raining. We pull up in front of the quaint house of Mr. Bennett, and I'm excited to talk to someone who understands. I help my grandma unload the groceries and we enter the home. "Tim!" my grandma calls as we enter the house.

We get no reply. "He must be asleep still," my grandma tells me.

I follow her down the long, wooden hall into the kitchen, where I set the bags on the counter. I go to the fridge and pour Mr. Bennett a glass of apple juice, his favorite morning drink. "I will go wake him up," I say to my grandma as she begins to unload the groceries. I casually walk down to the end of the hall where Mr. Bennett's room is. I turn the light on and prepare to say good morning, but then I see the bed. It is nicely made...and empty.

Surely he hasn't left the house alone. He never does that. I walk back down the hall and into the living room. I see Mr. Bennett sleeping in his favorite armchair. I smile and walk into the room. "Good morning!" I call in a singsong voice, but Mr. Bennett doesn't move. "Mr. Bennett," I whisper, approaching the old man. "Mr. Bennett?" He still doesn't wake up.

Then I shake him lightly. He still doesn't wake. I shake him harder. Nothing. Then I feel tears rushing to my eyes. I stumble backward, running into the table behind me, and drop the cup of juice. It splashes onto the floor. "Grandma!" I scream, clutching the table for support. "Grandma, come quickly!"

Everything after that comes in a blur. The paramedics come, followed by the police and a fire truck. I guess our neighborhood should be getting used to the sound of sirens. My grandma tells me to leave the house, so I wait in the yard, pacing back and forth. My mind is racing. Mr. Bennett can't be dead. He just can't be. I cannot think straight.

By now neighbors begin to gather near the home to see what is going on, but the police hold them back. They don't want bystanders. I sink down against a tree in Mr. Bennett's yard. Then I wait for what is to happen next.

I see the Maylores approaching the group. They look just as confused as everyone else. Marc looks like he has just gotten up. Dark circles are under his eyes. I try to look him in the eye, but right then the screen door rushes open. I turn toward it. I see two paramedics carrying a stretcher. A black sheet is draped over it. My grandma follows the group. Her eyes look shiny.

Right as the stretcher is being carried across the yard, I see Marc push through the crowd. He tries to run toward Mr. Bennett. His grandpa calls for him to come back, but he doesn't listen. Two policemen, who were called to the scene, rush over to him to keep him back. "No, wait!" he screams but the police don't let him budge. I see tears begin to rush from his eyes.

I stand up to watch Mr. Bennett being loaded into the ambulance. The paramedics slam the van doors. I feel myself begin to cry again.

The police let go of Marc as the van pulls away. Marc tries to run to it, but ends up sinking to the ground, hysterical. I want to go comfort him, but I can't seem to move. I watch my grandma and his grandparents rush to his side. He doesn't seem to notice; he just buries his face in his hands.

I have seen enough. I turn from the crowd and walk toward the lake.

<hr />

Mr. Bennett's funeral is held one week after his death. The doctors say that Mr. Bennett died peacefully in his sleep. My grandma tells me that he must have been ready to move on. I can't see why. He was in great health and had dozens of people who cared for him here, especially Marc.

I haven't seen Marc since that day last week. My family is pretty shaken by the awful turn of events, so I can't imagine how he must feel. To Marc, Mr. Bennett was like a second grandpa, maybe even a father figure. I thought of going to visit Marc several days ago, but I couldn't move myself to do it. Marc probably needs time, and after our last conversation, I'm probably the last person he wants to see.

The other bad news is that I have to go home in three days. My parents called my grandparents a couple of days ago saying they want Matt and me to come home so we can go to the LA premiere of my dad's new film. Normally Matt and I would be excited, but with everything that has happened, neither of us wants to go, even if we do get to walk a red carpet.

My grandma has made most of the arrangements for today. The service will be held at the small cemetery outside of town. I can't say I'm very excited for it. In my room I finish curling my hair. I'm wearing a plain black dress. It falls right above my knees. I also wear simple black heels. Since it is raining, I complete the outfit with a black cardigan. The weather has been bad since last week. Every day we seem to get rain. I was hoping today would be different.

I go downstairs. My grandparents prepare to leave with Matt, who I managed to dress up in a black button-up and slacks. They are going early to make sure everything is set up.

"You look very nice," my grandma says as I walk into the room.

"Thanks," I mutter back.

"Are you sure you want to take the truck on your own out to the cemetery?" she asks me.

I nod. "Yes, there is one stop I need to make first. Then I'll be right along."

"Okay, well, we need to get going. Lock up the house behind you and don't be late."

I watch them load into the car and pull out of the drive. Once they are gone I grab the keys to the truck and an umbrella. I start the old red truck up and pull out of the drive, but instead of turning left toward the main road, I take a right and continue down the street.

I stop in front of Mr. Bennett's house. It hasn't been touched since last week, although my grandma claims that after today she and some other neighbors will begin packing his stuff up. The rain has picked up. I open my umbrella and run out of the car and up the porch steps. I fumble with the key I took from my grandma, but eventually I make it into the house.

Once I'm in I close the umbrella and the door behind me. Then I stand, looking down the wood-paneled hall. The house seems so empty and has lost its warm, inviting feel. I slowly make my way down the hall and into the living room. My heels click across the wooden floor. I pause in the doorway, looking at the empty arm-chair. I see the glass I dropped on the ground, still there, lying empty.

I force myself to walk into the room. I sense the room's desolation. Then I make my way over to the shelves. I find Mr. Bennett's book and pull it down. I flip through it for the last time, looking at the pictures of his wife and things he loved. He said this book was important to him, and that it was something he would have forever. I'm going to make sure what Mr. Bennett said remains true. I'm going to take the book to his funeral so he has it forever.

As I near the end of the book, I stop. It seems thicker than it used to be. I flip to the last page. Just days ago the page was empty, but now it has been filled. I sink to my knees in bewilderment. Tears fill my eyes. On the last page of the book, Mr. Bennett has taped in the three pictures we took the other day. I see the one of Marc, the one of the three of us, and lastly the one of me. Did he really like me enough to put me in his book?

I begin to cry harder, partially out of sadness, but mostly because someone cared enough about me to remember me forever... I run my fingers over the picture, instantly missing Mr. Bennett. There is suddenly so much I want to tell him, yet I will never get the chance.

I sit on the ground for several more minutes, staring at the pictures, until I get hold of myself. Then I check the time on the wall. I have to get going. I stand up and fix my dress. Then I go to the bathroom and wipe my eyes. I try to make it look like I haven't been crying, but there isn't much I can do other than remove the smeared makeup. My eyes are already red and blotchy.

With the book clutched under my arm, I run back out into the rain to the truck.

⸻))((((⸻

By the time I get to the cemetery, people have already begun arriving. The rain has stopped, at least for the moment, but the clouds are still thick and heavy. I park the red truck in the back row and get out, still holding the book. People walk toward the entrance. Behind the perfectly kept tombstones is a large white tent. That is where the service will be held. I sigh and begin to walk toward the nicely trimmed grass.

"Aly!"

I turn to see Scott walking toward me. Slightly behind him, I see the rest of the Maylore family. Marc looks at the ground, making sure not to look at me.

"Haven't seen you in a while!" Scott calls.

"Yeah." I fake smile back. "I've been kind of busy," I say, even though I have done absolutely nothing in the course of the week.

"Us too," he replies. By now Marc's grandparents have caught up to us. "Hello, Alyson," they both greet me. I say hello back. Marc has now taken his eyes off the ground and has looked up, but he doesn't say anything.

His grandma nudges him. "Hi, Aly," he mumbles, not making eye contact. He's still mad at me and sad about what has happened, and I don't blame him.

"Are your grandparents here?" Mr. Maylore asks.

"I think they got here a while ago. They had to finish setting up."

Marc's grandma says she will see me inside.

I smile and nod. They begin walking again. "Marc!" I blurt out as he turns to leave. He stops and looks at me. His grandparents keep walking. It is now that I get a good look at Marc. His golden brown hair, which is usually swished over his eyebrows, has been intentionally tousled to the side, yet he still looks nice and put together. He wears a dark blue button-up with rolled-up sleeves and tan slacks. Obviously he is shying away from the all-black, depressed, funeral look.

"Here," I say, holding out the book.

"What's this?"

"Mr. Bennett said he always wanted this book to be with him."

Marc takes the book from me.

"Look at the last page," I say as I begin to walk away.

After I take several steps, I glance back to see Marc looking at the last page. I smile to myself and keep walking.

Inside the tent dozens of chairs have been set up. A small podium stands at the front, and behind that a slideshow of pictures that our street has compiled of Mr. Bennett plays in the background.

I see Chloe inside. She thanks me for saving her grandparents' stuff. Then the two of us sit down in the fourth row and wait for the service to start. My grandma and a few others stand on the podium to say some words. I don't really listen though. My mind wanders.

I remember the first time I met Mr. Bennett, and I remember the first time I actually talked to Marc Maylore, apart from when he ran into me in town. Both events occurred on the same day, at the same time, in the same house. I remember I stormed out of the house, angry and selfish. I then remember dinner with Mr. Bennett and how he brought Marc and me back together again. He was the one we went to after we made up. In fact, the more I think of it, the more I realize that Mr. Bennett not only played an important part in my summer; he also played a crucial role in my friendship with Marc. The thought of him not being here makes me sick to my stomach. Then again, even if he were here, I don't think Marc and I will ever have the same relationship we had before.

Then I hear the speaker change and I look up to see who it is. Marc. I sit up in my chair. Marc taps the microphone, sending little cracks of noise into the room.

"Thank you all for coming. I know Mr. Timothy Bennett would be honored that all of you came out today. That so many of you cared about him. I don't want to say much, but there is something I would like you all to remember: Mr. Bennett was a friend to all. Never once in the years I knew him did he have an enemy or a person he disliked. He wanted to get to know everyone in the best way possible. He was kind, caring, and compassionate to everyone. I never once saw him mad or unhappy. He tried to make the best of everything.

"I learned a lot from Mr. Bennett, but there are three particular lessons that I have never forgotten. Mr. Bennett always told me that you have to fight for what you believe in, you have to make sacrifices for what you want, and when you mess up, you have to try to fix it. We are only ourselves once, so why not try to make our life the best it can possibly be?" He pauses and at that moment looks directly at me. I realize these are not only Mr. Bennett's words; Marc is talking to me. He is teaching me this lesson.

"I know that Mr. Bennett would be honored if we all tried to live by his words of wisdom. I know that he would feel he made an impact on our small community. So I challenge you, next time the going gets tough or you feel lost, think of what Timothy Bennett said, and try to live life to the fullest. Thank you."

Marc quickly exits the podium. I can't help but smile. When the next speaker has taken the podium, Marc turns around from a couple of rows in front of me. He mouths at me, "We need to talk."

I nod.

—————— «(|)» ——————

After the service has ended, Marc comes and finds me. In the time we have been in the tent, the sun has come out, lighting the whole sky and sending a yellow glow onto the small cemetery. "Very nice speech," my grandma applauds as Marc approaches us in the parking lot.

"Thank you, Mrs. Henderbell."

"Grandma, is it okay if Marc and I go talk for a little bit? I have the truck and I will be back before dinner tonight."

She looks at Marc. "Are your grandparents okay with that?"

He nods. "As long as I make it back for the dinner, I'm good."

"All right, then it's okay with me, but please make sure you are there when the meal starts. I don't want you kids showing up late to Mr. Bennett's memorial dinner."

"We won't. I promise," I say.

Marc and I turn to leave the group. "Where's the book?" I ask him.

"With Mr. Bennett," he quietly replies.

I smile, instantly glad I made the extra stop this morning.

"I'm sorry about what happened. This must be an awful time for you..." I say as we approach the old red truck. "I was going to come see you."

"Don't worry about it," he replies. "I probably would have made you leave if you came near my house."

I smile. "It just takes time..."

"Lots of it," Marc agrees. "Although I don't know how I will ever get over his death."

"Well," I say, choosing my words carefully, "don't think of Mr. Bennett as a loss. Instead think of him as someone who just had to go. Think of him for all he taught you. Remember him for what he told you. Don't reflect over what you never got to do or what you missed. He was always optimistic and strong, and you are too."

"I know. It's just hard," he replies, getting in the passenger seat.

"I know how you feel." I start the engine. It roars to life and I pull out of the parking lot. "Where are we going?"

"I know a good place." He guides me onto the right roads. We drive in silence until we arrive at what looks to be the outside of a forest.

"Where are we?" I ask.

"The National Forest," he replies.

We enter and he directs me to a small dirt road that leads up to a small sandy beach and lake. I stop the car. "Wow," I say, stepping out. "It's so pretty..."

"It has always been one of my favorite places. Scott used to drive me out here when I was younger."

I slip off my heels and step into the soft sand. It feels cool under my feet. The lake is small. In fact, it might be closer to the size of a pond. Trees surround it. The afternoon sun sends beams across the water. This place is so surreal.

Marc walks toward the water and I follow him. "I'm sorry I couldn't explain to you why I knew the other night. I was just so caught up in the moment and shocked at what had happened, I couldn't find the words," he says, looking out at the water. "But

I can now. You see, I didn't really know until the night they were caught that Chris and Andrew were the robbers. I was in town at the hardware store that evening, getting some supplies for Scott, and they were there in the next aisle over. I overheard them talking about getting some type of wrench to take to the Colemans' that night. I didn't really think anything of it until I was out of the store. Then I realized that the Colemans were gone, and Chris and Andrew had no reason to go there in the dark unless they were the robbers. I kind of put two and two together, but I couldn't go to the police because I had no proof, so I decided to go out that night and get myself some evidence, like a picture. If I could prove it was them, then I could go to the police. That was my plan from the start, but obviously it was a failure..."

"But why were you yelling at them outside the restaurant that one day?"

"Oh that," he begins. "Well, the previous day Eric and I were hanging out by the lake and so were they. Once again I overheard them joking about the robbery. The next day I went to confront them and tell them that event was no joke, but they brushed it off. It made me mad how shallow and callous they were. I just feel stupid for not realizing then what they were up to."

"Well, I want to apologize too. I kept cutting you off and wouldn't let you explain. I was afraid that you were going to tell me you had known all along or had been a part of it, and I didn't want you to be a liar, not after I'd come to trust you. You're a good person, Marc, and I totally overreacted. I made this some huge misunderstanding."

"It's okay. What I said to you was harsh."

I walk up to him and stand by the water's edge. The water slowly laps up on the shore, splashing my toes and sending a cool sensation through my body.

"So are we good again?" I ask.

He nods. "I'm glad we talked things out. I kind of missed seeing you around." He smiles.

"Me too," I reply, "and to think that after that night I hoped I'd never talk to you again."

"I felt the same way."

We become silent. Then Marc speaks. "I'm going to Minneapolis tomorrow," he says. "I have to help start the basketball training camps for this year, since I'm the captain."

"When do you get back?" I ask, suddenly worried this is the last time I will get to see him.

"Well, I heard you are leaving on Monday, so I will be back by then. I'll leave tomorrow morning, stay two days, and then make it back late morning on Monday to say good-bye."

"So this is the last time we really get to spend any time together..." I say quietly.

He nods. "So we have to make the best of it."

"You don't have to come back on Monday if you don't want... just to say good-bye."

"But I want to," he replies, smiling.

"Is Eric going?"

"No, he gets to do the next one."

"I'm going to miss it here," I say.

"I'm going to miss having you here."

"I'll come and visit every break I get."

"Enough sad talk," he says, splashing me.

"Hey!" I yell, jumping back. "Not again! We have a dinner to go to!"

"Oh, screw the wet clothes. We will change before we go. We have plenty of time!"

I laugh and splash him back. The two of us run into the shallow water, splashing each other any chance we can get. We are like five-year-olds. Marc picks me up and spins me in the water, then throws me out into the cool liquid. I laugh. We continue our fun until I begin to get cold.

We run back to shore dripping wet. I run over to the truck and dig around in the back for a sweatshirt. I find a big black one that must be my grandpa's and slip it on. "You cold?" I ask.

He shakes his head. "No, but do you have any music?"

I dig around in the glove box. "Here is a cassette tape. It doesn't say what songs are on it though."

"Play it anyway," Marc coaxes.

I stick the keys in the car and stick the tape in the tape player. The tape starts up with some horn solo. "Hey, I know this song." Marc laughs.

"You know this?"

"Yeah! It's an old one, but my grandparents sometimes play this music at home."

He puts his arm out, and I take it. Then he spins me. I come out of the spin perfectly balanced and I put my hands on his wet waist. "Hey, you actually landed your spin." He laughs.

"Yep," I say proudly. "Didn't end up in the water again, yet somehow we are wet." He chuckles and spins me again. "We should enter some ballroom dancing competition."

"Totally."

The song comes to a close and we collapse onto the sand. I rest my head on his shoulder, and the two of us stare out at the water. We sit there in silence, just enjoying each other's company.

"What time is it?" I ask, stretching my feet out into the sand a little while later.

Marc gets up and goes to the car to check the time. "Aly..." he calmly says.

"Yeah?" I say, turning around.

"It's 6:40. We have twenty minutes."

I just look at him, and then I am on my feet. "Twenty minutes! We can't make it back to the house to change in time!"

"I know."

"We just need to go..."

"I know, I'll drive."

We run to the car and hop in. He quickly drives out of the parking lot. In the car I use the cracked overhead mirror to try to put myself together. My hair is almost dry, but it is knotted. Luckily I have a small brush in my bag. I brush it out and throw it into a ponytail. Then I try my best to brush the sand from my dress, though it doesn't really come off. I slip my heels back on. And put on my damp cardigan over my damp dress. "How do I look?" I ask, though I know I look awful.

"Great," Marc says, putting a smile on his face.

In town Marc parks the truck. I hop out and wait for him to put on his shoes and tuck in his shirt. He runs his fingers through his hair. The two of us walk into the restaurant looking confident.

When my grandma sees us, partially wet and sandy, she doesn't even ask us what happened. She just sighs and walks away.

When she is gone, Marc and I can't help but look at ourselves and burst into laughter.

CHAPTER 16

My last three days go by in a blur. I talk with my grandparents. I spend time with Chloe and Eric, but it feels weird that Marc isn't here. I swim, Jet Ski, and boat as much as I can. I try my best to enjoy every last second of the trip. Even though I am going home, I feel like I am about to leave home. I'm going to miss everyone here and all they have taught me.

On the night before Matt and I depart, I get a call from my mom... Well, actually Matt does. The two of them talk for a while and then Matt hands the phone to me. I just look at him. He nods, coaxing me to take the phone. I take a deep breath and answer it. "Hello?"

"Hi, Alyson," my mom's voice says back. This time she doesn't sound busy. "How are you?"

"Fine."

"I'm very sorry to hear about Timothy Bennett. I met him and his wife once."

"You did?"

"Yes," she replied, "he was such a kind person. He will be missed."

"He will be," I quietly say.

"Your father and I are looking forward to seeing you," she tells me.

"You are?" I say, a hint of astonishment in my voice.

"Well, yes! Just because we send you away to learn a lesson doesn't mean we don't care about you. We have missed you dearly."

"Oh," I say, not sure how to reply.

"You know what you did was wrong, and I want you to understand we just wanted what was best for you. I'm sure we messed up too along the way, but I just can't watch my daughter become someone she isn't. I hope we made the right choice..."

"You did," I reply. I never thought I would say that, but at that moment my grandparents, Matt, Marc, Chloe, and Eric flash through my mind. Without them I would have never learned who I really was. I would have never learned to trust, love, and feel loved again. I have finally learned to accept that I messed up. "I'm sorry I snuck out and stole the money. I was stupid..."

"It's okay, Alyson—part of growing up is making mistakes." She pauses. "I'll let you finish packing. See you tomorrow!"

"Bye, Mom," I reply, utterly shocked that we had this conversation.

Then at the last second, right before she hangs up, I hear my mom say something I never thought I would hear again: "I love you."

Then the call ends.

I sit on my bed staring at the lake. Maybe going home won't be so bad after all.

———————

Morning comes around, and everyone gathers in the driveway to say good-bye. I say good-bye to Dr. Meyers, the Blaires, and Scott. I say good-bye to the Maylores and the Colemans.

When it is Chloe's turn to say good-bye, she gives me a hug. "I'm going to miss you and your fashion advice and our fun times."

I hug her back. "I'll miss you too, but I'll be back as soon as I can." We let go and look at each other.

"I might go look at colleges in California. Maybe we can see each other when I come?"

"Of course!" I reply. "You can stay at my place! And we can still keep in touch! There is always the good old-fashioned phone call. Plus, I get my cell phone back when I get home, so we can text."

"Sounds good to me." She smiles, stepping back so Eric can say good-bye.

"Bye, Chloe."

I look over at Eric. "Bye, Aly," he says, giving me a quick hug.

"Hey, thanks for all the crazy good times." I laugh.

"It's what I do." He grins.

"Bye, Eric."

I look at my grandparents. "We better get going if you want to make the flight," my grandma says.

"Can't we just wait another minute?" I ask. "Marc is supposed to be here."

"Maybe he couldn't get away," my grandpa says, putting his hand on my shoulder.

"We really need to go, honey," my grandma says.

"Okay," I whisper. Matt and I get into the car. Maybe he wasn't going to come at all. Maybe he got held up in traffic. I sigh. There is always the phone, I think sadly to myself.

My grandpa starts up the engine. I look at Matt. "Ready to leave?" I ask.

He shakes his head. "I'll never be ready."

"Me neither," I say, taking one last look at the house as we drive down the road.

It isn't good-bye forever. I will be back soon. But for now it seems like forever, and that is hard enough. What makes it ten times worse is I didn't get to say good-bye to Marc.

The car is quiet. My grandparents are sad to see us go, and we are sad too. No one knows what to say or do.

As we turn off the road onto the small two-lane highway, I look out the window. We pass the many trees of the forest. I'm going to miss the forest. Suddenly I see something in the road ahead. "What's that?" I ask.

"It looks like a car..." my grandpa says, sounding concerned and slowing down. As we get closer, I realize my grandpa is right. It looks as if a car has driven off the road into one of the big trees down below.

"Stop the car!" I yell. My grandparents and Matt look at me. "That's Marc's Range Rover..." I whisper.

My grandpa slams on his brakes. "You two stay here," he tells Matt and me.

But I don't listen, and I jump out of the car too. My heart is pounding and I'm breathing heavily. I follow my grandpa around the front of the car. The hood of the car has smashed into the tree. Branches and shattered glass from the windshield are everywhere.

The airbags have deployed. My grandpa turns and looks at me, and then up at my grandma. She is on the phone, calling 911. My grandpa asks me, "How could he have driven off the road like this?"

I feel sick to my stomach. Marc must have been driving fast, as usual, to make it back in time to see me. I stumble backward, falling onto the glass-covered ground.

My grandpa rushes to my side. "Alyson, are you okay?"

I nod. "Where is he?"

My grandpa stands back up and walks over to the car. "He isn't here," he says, scratching his head, confused. "He couldn't have gone far..."

I look over toward the forest. *Could you have been any stupider, Marc?* Then I see blood in the grass in front of me. "I know where he is!" I scream, and then I take off running into the forest.

My grandpa calls for me to come back, but I don't listen. Marc was trying to get help, and the quickest way back to the houses is through the forest. I stay close to the ground looking for any more splotches of blood. "Marc!" I yell. "Marc!" Then I see more blood on the lush green grass and I follow it, calling for Marc the whole time. My heart is racing. I can't stay calm.

I feel like I am chasing the robbers again. I run fast, and blindly, for I have no clue where I'm going. He can't be much farther away. "Marc!" I scream again. And then I see him.

He is ahead of me, propped up against a large oak tree. "Oh my God, Marc!" I cry, running to his side. He gives a weak smile when he sees me. He doesn't look good. Scrapes from the shattered glass are spread all over his body. A large gash is above his eyebrow, and blood slowly oozes over his eye. He clutches his side with one arm. Broken ribs, I think. I then look down to his leg. It is twisted in a weird position, behind his bloodstained shorts.

"Marc," I whisper, running my hand over his forehead and pushing his hair to the side.

"I wrecked the car..." he whispers back.

I nod. "You were driving fast again..." I say, tears beginning to well in my eyes.

"As usual...there was a bunny in the road. I tried not to hit it," he replies, trying to laugh, but he ends up grimacing in pain.

His eyes look colorless, and I can tell it won't be long before he loses consciousness. "The ambulance is on its way," I say. "Just focus on me." I try to stay calm, but my body starts to shake. I grab Marc's hand. He squeezes it back, hard, probably trying to relieve some of the pain.

"I'm sorry you have to see me this way," he whispers. "I kind of hoped our good-bye would be a little bit more...exciting," he slowly says.

"Oh Marc." A tear slips from my eye.

"Are you going to LA?"

I nod.

"The basketball team looks good this year," he tells me. "Coach says I'm in for a great season..."

"Good."

Marc tries to close his eyes. I'm no doctor, but I think this is bad. "Keep your eyes on me," I tell him.

"There's something I want to tell you," he says.

"And what's that?"

"I want to thank you for all that you did for me this summer..."

I smile. "What do you mean?"

He pauses. "You're a good person, Aly."

"So are you," I reply, wishing I could get more out of him.

He takes a deep breath, trying to grasp enough air to say something else. "Aly, thank you." He pauses, trying hard to form words.

"Thank you for what?" I ask, squeezing his hand tighter and looking into his eyes, fearing I will never know what he is thanking me for.

"For everything..." and then he blacks out.

I sit on the roadside next to my grandparents' car. My grandpa is talking to one of the policemen who have arrived at the scene. The paramedics have just hauled off Marc in an ambulance.

I turn away from everything, the messed-up car, my grandpa, the cops looking through the wreckage, and I just stare down at the ground and concentrate on my breathing. I take a slow breath in and then slowly let it out. I try to keep myself under control, but the horrific scene is beginning to catch up with me. I lose it. I begin to bawl. Tears run out of my eyes. Makeup runs down my face. I'm blinded by my tears and paralyzed in anxiety. I can't quite seem to catch my breath.

This is all my fault. If he hadn't wanted to come back, if I had done something to stop his driving habit, he wouldn't have gotten hurt. Marc was driving back to see me, and if he hadn't...

I begin to cry harder, if that is even possible, and then I feel someone giving me a hug, but I don't look up. "Aly, everything is going to be okay," my little brother says. "Shhh, just take a deep breath." I feel him gently rubbing my back.

"We can't go back. I won't go...not today," I sob.

"I know..." he says. "I know."

I sit in a grassy field overlooking the little creek that runs out of the lake. It's dusk, and the sky is filled with an array of oranges and purples. This is the spot Chloe wanted to take me the first night I arrived, when I was "grounded."

We didn't go to the airport, not after what happened. We would have missed our flight anyway. My grandparents felt it would be an awful idea for us to go back to LA so soon after Marc's accident.

Instead we went to the hospital, where Marc was being fixed up. The doctors were keeping a close eye on him, and he wasn't allowed any visitors, not even his grandparents. I could only sit in a hospital waiting room for so long before I had to get out. So I left and went back to the house.

A bird calls in the distance, and the reeds of the creek sway back and forth in the gentle breeze. I stare off into the void, not noticing anything. I'm still traumatized by the day's events. I can't close my eyes without seeing Marc's bloodied body and empty eyes staring into mine.

I clutch a bottle in my hand, and then take a sip from it. The liquid inside tastes disgusting and I force myself to swallow it, but it keeps me from crying. Right now, I just want to forget. I take another swig from the bottle and set it back in the grass.

"What're you doing?" I suddenly hear a voice ask.

I turn around to see Eric standing behind me.

"Enjoying this one hell of day," I say in a harsh, sarcastic tone. I take another sip from the bottle and make a face as I force it down. "How did you find me?"

"I saw you leave the house. I was on my way over. I needed someone to talk to. I saw you leave..."

He sits down beside me in the grass and stretches his legs out in front of him. He then looks over at me and raises his eyebrows.

"Want some?" I ask.

He nods and takes the bottle. He takes a rather big sip and effortlessly swallows it. Then, taking the bottle with him, he stands up and dumps the liquid out of the bottle out into the nearby grass. He comes back and sits down.

"Hey, what was that for?" I ask.

"Saving us from a headache tomorrow. I don't think getting drunk is the answer to our problems."

I just look at him.

"Where did you get that?" he asks.

"My grandparents' garage, in a cabinet... They aren't supposed to know it is gone."

"I know nothing," Eric says, putting his hands in a surrendering motion.

I smile.

"So what exactly were you trying to do with that?" he asks.

"I was trying to forget," I simply reply, looking away. "I was trying to forget today."

"You really thought that would work?"

"No, but I used to do it sometimes at home."

The trees sway slightly in the light breeze. I shiver in the leather jacket I haven't worn in weeks.

"Well, good thing I showed up."

"I used to go to a lot of parties...that's how I would forget. At home the drinks taste better," I quietly reply.

"Yeah, Marc mentioned you said you used to party a lot."

"He did?"

"Well, only after I asked him. It wasn't hard to tell, Butler."

"Did Marc tell you that was part of the reason that I came?"

He nods. "We were all going to find out at some point. The clues just kept adding up. Don't blame Marc for spilling; he just confirmed."

"I won't," I reply.

"You know he cares a lot about you. You are one of his best friends." Eric smiles.

It is then that I feel a tear slip down my face.

"Aly," Eric says, suddenly looking concerned, "Marc is going to be okay. He will be just fine."

"Was it my fault?" I say, choking on my tears.

"Your fault?"

"I mean, he was coming to see me... I knew he would be cutting it close to make it here on time... I should have just said good-bye a couple days ago. He didn't need to see me off."

"He wanted to see you off just as much as you did," Eric replies.

"Well, if I had just done something to help with his driving problem..."

"Ha. Trust me, I tried to stop that when he first got his license."

"You know he drives like that?" I ask.

"Hello, I'm his best friend. I'm not blind," he replies. "Plus I ride with him a lot."

"I wish I would have done something."

"He wouldn't have listened. It's how he clears his mind. Aly, you have to promise me, promise Marc, you will stop blaming yourself. Right this very second. The last thing Marc needs is to feel guilty because you feel it is your fault. When he wakes up, he is going to have other problems to deal with."

Eric, the kid who is always so easygoing, so funny, suddenly looks extremely serious. He stares right into my eyes. "You have to promise me."

I nod, looking away to hold back tears. "I promise."

We fall silent for several minutes. I hear the creek gurgle around the small rocks. I hear some kid yelling at his dad from the road above. More birds start to say their good nights, and the crickets begin to say their hellos.

"God, why did this happen to Marc?" Eric finally says. "Why did this have to happen?" He stands up and kicks the ground, sending grass and dirt spinning into the air. He picks up one of the small rocks in the grass and with all his strength sends it flying into the creek. It splashes and sinks. Several more rocks are thrown before Eric finally crouches down and covers his face.

"Eric," I quietly say, walking toward him, but he cuts me off.

"It should have been me. Marc has so much going for him... He has so much potential. What do I have?"

"Stop it, Eric," I say, putting my hand on his shoulder. "What's done is done. There's nothing we can do to change the situation. We just need to calm down and be there for Marc. Besides, you told me not to blame myself. You can't blame yourself either."

That's easier said than done though, because it's blatantly obvious both Eric and I are freaking out.

Eric looks at me. His face is bright red. "Maybe we should go see him."

"Tonight? We can't," I say, assuming visitor hours are over. Not to mention that earlier, even his own family wasn't allowed in to see him.

"It's worth a shot," he says, standing up.

I follow him toward his old red Jeep.

"Thank you for showing up tonight, Eric." I smile, walking beside him.

"You're welcome," he replies, unlocking the car.

———— ((●)) ————

By the time we reach the big hospital three towns over, the sky is almost completely black. Giant overhead lights in the parking lot guide us to a sliding glass door with the word *EMERGENCY* flashing across the top of it.

The waiting room is dimly lit. It's practically empty. I guess my grandparents and Matt must have left. Only one man sits in one of the chairs reading a magazine while a woman quietly naps in the corner. Eric tells me to wait by the chairs while he talks to the receptionist about seeing Marc. I slide into a chair and begin to feel nervous. Nervous about what Marc will look like if I see him. Nervous about what he will say, nervous about what he will do. I tap my fingers on the arm of the waiting room chair.

"Aly?" I look up to see Eric beside me. "You okay? I called your name like three times."

"Yeah, sorry, I was just thinking..."

"Visiting hours are over. Only immediate family can see Marc. They won't let us back. Not tonight. Probably not tomorrow either."

A feeling of disappointment suddenly comes over me. Eric must see this because he sits down in the chair next to me. "Hey, there will be plenty of time to see Marc. It's probably best that he gets his rest right now. He probably wouldn't want to see us anyway." Eric puts a smile on his face, but I can see he is upset too.

Together we slowly begin to head to the door. I can't believe Marc is so close yet so far away. But then I hear a familiar voice.

"Eric! Aly!" We turn around to see Marc's grandma walking into the waiting room. "I was wondering when you two would show up." She looks tired and concerned, but she smiles in our presence.

"Yeah, we were just coming to stop by, but we found out visiting hours are over..." Eric says, shoving his hands in his pocket.

"Technically they are, but you can come back with me if you want. I was just taking a little walk outside the room. I'll 'sneak' you back."

"Mrs. Maylore, that is very kind of you to offer, but I don't want to disrupt Marc," I say, though I desperately want to see him.

"He is asleep, my dear; you wouldn't bug him at all. Besides, my husband would like a familiar face to talk to. You see, Marc's parents are on their way from Minneapolis, so it has just been the two of us and Scott."

"Well, if you're sure it won't disrupt you and the doctors," I say.

"I insist you two come back with me," she replies as she begins to head back toward the hallway from where she has just come. "You are as close to immediate family as we are."

Marc's grandparents leave the small hospital room so Eric and I can see Marc without being cramped.

"Now remember, kids," Mr. Maylore begins, "Marc has a lot of healing to do, but he's in great hands and will be perfectly fine."

"Yes sir," Eric replies, "we know."

I nod, take a deep breath, and push open the door.

The room is softly lit. It's silent too, except for the occasional low beep of a machine they have Marc hooked up to.

I look over at him. He is asleep. His leg is in a cast and is elevated above the bed. He has an IV stuck in his arm and an oxygen mask over his nose. It lightly fogs up when he exhales. He has stitches above his eyebrow, in addition to several places on his arm. He is also covered in bandages.

I want to cry when I see him, but not because of all the injuries. I want to cry because after all he has been through, he looks peaceful. He is tucked under a blue blanket, arms at his side. His eyes are closed, and his golden brown hair sweeps gently across his forehead. His chest slowly moves up and down as he breathes. Minus the bandages, Marc still looks somewhat put together.

"Oh Marc…" I whisper as a single tear escapes my eye.

Then, Eric and I stand there in silence for what seems like forever. I don't really have anything to say, and I don't think Eric does either. We just want to be silent and appreciate the time we have with Marc.

Eric finally takes a step toward Marc's hospital bed. "Hey, buddy," he whispers, "it could have been a lot worse. I mean, think about it, you could have broken both legs, or had one amputated, or had them both…"

"Eric," I say, cutting him off.

He looks back at me, a slight grin appearing on his face. "Sorry, but, hey, even though I probably look like an idiot talking to a sleeping person right now, I just want you to know that when you wake up, I will be here for you. I always have been and I always will." He takes a step back and puts his hands in his pockets. "That's all I have to say. I think I'm going to step into the waiting room." He looks over at me. "Take your time," he says, walking toward the door.

"I'll be there in a minute."

I look at Marc lying serenely in the bed. I walk over and sit down in a chair beside him. I put my hands in my lap and fidget in the chair for a minute, trying to get comfortable.

"I know you will never hear this, because, well, you are totally out of it, but since we never got our good-bye…" I trail off and then start back up again. "Marc, you are one of the people I find easiest to talk to. From the day I first spoke to you on your back porch, I was amazed at how I felt I could open up to you. I had just met you, and I wanted to tell you my life's story.

"I had a blast this summer, and it's all because of you. I was going off the deep end. I can admit that now. I was partying all the time, doing things I shouldn't have. I even stole from my own parents. When I arrived, I wanted nothing to do with this place, but when I met you, I suddenly wanted to act like a different person. I wanted to act like the person I know I really can be. I want to thank you for bringing me back to reality, because that is why my parents wanted me to come up here to Minnesota." I pause, biting my tongue. "I'm so sorry this happened to you. Eric is right, you don't deserve this, but I'm here for you too, like you were here for me."

I sniffle and look away for a minute to wipe my tears away. Why am I so emotional? I look back to the sleeping Marc, but this time I see a pair of sparkling blue eyes staring back at me.

"Marc," I whisper, laughing through my tears. I reach for his hand, squeezing it. It is warm and full of life.

"Hi, Aly," he says, though his voice is barely a whisper.

"Hi, Marc." I smile. "See, we knew you were going to be okay."

Right as I say that, the door opens, and a doctor walks into the room. Marc's grandma is behind him. "Miss Butler, I need to ask that you leave. There are some tests that need to be run on Mr. Maylore."

I take one last look at Marc lying in the hospital bed. "Bye, Marc," I say as Mrs. Maylore escorts me out of the room.

I look back to see a small smile form on his face.

This will be the last time I see Marc Maylore this summer, and though hard to accept, I finally feel like I got a proper good-bye.

CHAPTER 17

I sit in the window seat in my large, luxurious room. The only source of light comes from the single lamp beside my four-poster bed. I quietly tap my fingers against the cool windowpane. The clock on my bedside table says 12:45 a.m. I have been home for twenty-four hours. Matt and I left the morning after the car crash. It was the only flight we could get back to LA in time to attend my dad's movie premiere.

My grandparents called Matt and me that evening to tell us Marc had woken up for longer periods throughout the day. They also said there were no serious injuries other than a broken leg, broken ribs, and a concussion. He wouldn't have any permanent damage if he took the time to heal.

My home seems distant, like a strange place. It feels big and lonely. My parents are out at a party for my dad's new film. They said they would stay home with us, keep us company, but I told them to go. They deserve to, and besides, there is nothing they can do to make me feel better. My siblings are asleep. It's only me, and for the first time in a long time, I feel lost.

I think of the safe sitting in the basement, the place where my whole mess began. I've been avoiding that area of the house since I returned.

I run my hand over the shiny latch on the window. I got my cell phone back, and Tiffany texted me saying there was going to be a big party at the beach all night. I could go check it out. All the good stuff doesn't start until late anyway. It would be so easy to go, just forget everything. I don't think I would get caught, but if I did... I push that terrible thought out of my mind.

I step back off the window seat and open the window. The deep, smoggy California air seeps into my bedroom. It seems heavier than the fresh air at the lake. I hear sirens and a car horn out in the distance. I see no stars in the sky and hear no water gently lapping up against the shore. I sit back down on the seat, contemplating whether I should go out.

"I wouldn't do that if I were you," a voice behind me says.

I turn to see Matt standing in my doorway. I haven't even heard him open the door. "Do what?"

"You're better than that," he says, joining me on the large window seat.

"Why are you up?" I ask him.

"Too much running through my mind, I guess. And I heard you up and about."

Matt pushes the window closed. Then he gets up, walks into the bathroom, and pours me a cup of water. He sets it in front of me and sits back down. "Drink this," he tells me. I drink the whole glass.

When I'm finished, he begins to talk again. "You realize Marc is going to be okay, right? Don't freak out and fall back into your old habits."

"What if Marc isn't okay though? What if he isn't the same again?" I look at the clock again. 12:52.

"Are you the same person you were two months ago?"

I shake my head. "I changed myself... This could change him."

"No, you didn't. Do you honestly think you would have changed your lifestyle if you hadn't been caught?"

I look at him.

"You see, sometimes events change us for the better."

"Or worse," I mutter.

"It could, but it depends on the perspective you take toward it. I know things look bad now, but they will get better in time. Everything happens for a reason, Aly."

"I guess," I reply.

"But for now, you have to stay positive. You have to stay strong. You changed. You made better decisions. You can't let that all slip away now because of what has happened. You have to face life, not hide from it, and I'm pretty sure you have been hiding from it for a very long time."

I look at my younger brother, so wise, so mature. "You're right, Matt. I have to be better."

A smile forms across his face. "We all believe in you. I do, Marc does, Chloe and Eric, Grandma and Grandpa, even Mom and Dad. I mean, think about it; you were fine yesterday. Do you really think Marc would like to hear that you returned to partying and stealing money just because of something that happened to him?"

I shake my head.

"We trust you to make the right decisions, Aly." He pauses. "We trust you."

Those words send shivers through my body. I never thought I would hear them again after what I did. Ever. I smile.

"You know what Grandma told me?" Matt asks me.

"What?"

"Moments in life define us, but it is our choice as to who we become."

"She told me that too," I quietly reply.

"Think about it. It kind of makes sense. Now come on, let's go get some sleep. We will be back in Minnesota before you know it."

"I sure hope so," I say. He stands up. I do too, prepared to finally get in bed. Matt walks to the door, but then stops.

"Aly..."

"Yes, Matt."

"Here," he says, handing me an envelope.

I turn it over to see my name scrawled across the top in sloppy handwriting. "What is this?"

"I found it."

"Found it where?" I think I know where this is going.

Matt looks at me with a blank face.

"Matt..."

"I found it at the crash. It was lying in the grass by Marc's car. It was after the paramedics took him away and you were sitting by yourself on the curb. I took it. I planned on giving it to you later, when you weren't as upset, but I think you need to read it now."

"Did you read it?" I ask him.

He shakes his head. "My name isn't on the front." He pauses. "I know I shouldn't have picked it up, but I was afraid if I didn't, you would never get it."

"Thank you, Matt," I kindly reply, smiling.

"Good night, Aly," he says, but a moment later he sticks his head back into the room. "You know you really are the best sister, even if you get yourself into stupid things."

"Good night, Matt!"

With my room to myself, I look at the envelope. I trace my finger over my scribbled name. Marc wrote this before the accident. It might have even been one of the last things he did.

I stop thinking about it and tear open the covering. I pull out a piece of paper, folded into perfect thirds. I open it up and begin to read:

Dear Aly,

I know I probably seem pretty lame for writing a letter, because who does that these days? But since you don't have a phone or computer and I want to make sure you get this, I'm just going to hand-write this for reassurance you will ac-tually get to read it. I'm also writing this because as I look at the clock, I realize I probably will only make it back to the lake to say good-bye to you, not to talk, and there are some things I want to tell you before you go.

First off, we need to keep in touch. I don't care how, even if we have to write these "old fashioned" letters, but just send me a text every once in a while to let me know what you are up to. I will do the same. I feel we have experienced too much together to just stop talking. Plus, I don't want what happened to our parents to happen to us.

Secondly, I want to thank you. I know you are probably confused as to why because you didn't help me overcome anything or whatever...but you did have some good things to say. Even if you don't always live by your advice, you do give some great recommendations on living life. If it wasn't for you I would still probably be mad at Eric and afraid to look at my future and decide what I really want to do. You helped me get over my biggest fear, rejection, and learn how to accept it. There is something about the way you speak that makes me feel like what you say is actually important, and it is. At least I think so.

Also, thank you for believing in me all summer, even when you never wanted to speak to me again. Thank you for always finding your way back to me even when I made huge mistakes.

I know you want to credit me for helping you out this summer, but other than listen to you and keep you company, I think you helped yourself more than you know. You're a good person, Aly. You just have to figure out who you want to be, and I think you have. I think you just needed to meet someone who accepts you for whoever you want to be, and that is where I come in.

I know this is probably a really cliché, cheesy way to end this letter, but it is true. I just wanted to say I'm so glad to have met you this summer and call you my best friend. I can't wait to see you again, whether it is back at the lake or in California.

Until next time, Alyson Butler.
Your friend,
Marc Maylore

When I look up from the letter, I am in tears. I reread the letter for what seems like forever. When I finally stop, I've come to a conclusion: Matt and Grandma are right, and Marc's letter confirms it: *moments in life define us, but it is our choice as to who we become.*

CHAPTER 18

FOUR MONTHS LATER

The car rolls through the ice and slush of the road. On either side of me, soft blankets of snow cover the grass, the trees, and anything and everything visible. Long sheets of ice cover the once glistening lakes. The once lush forests, so full of life, have now become barren lands of bare trees and snow. The only life is the occasional rabbit passing by.

I lean my head on the frosty window. The cold windowpane sends shivers through my body. I shudder from the cold. It seems like I would be warm, wearing a long-sleeved shirt, sweater, parka, jeans, leg warmers, boots, gloves, and even a hat. But even in the warm car, the cold still gets to me. I guess that's what happens when you live in sunny California your whole life. I look over at Matt. He, too, is bundled up, but he doesn't look as cold as me. "You ready to be back?" he asks me.

I smile and nod.

"It is a little different this time of year," my grandpa says from the front seat of the car.

"I don't know how you manage to live in the cold for half of the year." I laugh.

"You learn to deal with it," my grandpa replies.

My parents allow Matt and me to spend winter break here. In fact, my parents, Jake, and Lily are even coming to town on the back end of the holiday so we can all be together. Matt and I begged from the moment we got home from Minnesota to go back, and winter break was the first possible moment. My grandparents are thrilled to hear that they will get to see everyone. For now though, it is just Matt and me, just like before.

We turn off the two-lane highway and onto the small dirt road that leads to the house. I eagerly look out the window, waiting for the house to appear, and then I see it. The white cottage is covered with a white blanket of snow. Long icicles hang from the roof. The yard looks much emptier than before, now that the trees have lost their leaves. Nevertheless, it still looks the same, and I am glad to be back. I open the car door. My feet crunch through the snow as I run toward the house for warmth. Matt follows, and so does my grandpa, carrying our two large suitcases.

When I make it into the entry hall, I take a deep breath. The heat is on and I instantly feel warmth sink through my heavy jacket. When my grandma hears the door, she comes out of the kitchen to greet us. "Alyson! Matthew!" She beams, giving us a hug. "You're here! How was your flight?"

I slip off my boots and follow her into the kitchen. "Good," I say.

"For someone who hates flying, it was fine," Matt replies.

The house smells of cinnamon and pies. It looks exactly the same, only this time there is a fire roaring in the stone fireplace in the living room. I crouch down beside it so I can feel the radiating heat on my face.

We all talk for a little bit, to get caught up. I tell my grandparents about school and applying for colleges, and Matt tells them about his year. Then they bring us up to speed on their lives in the quiet town of Davis Lake. It's just like how it used to be.

Eric, Chloe, and I all sit in a circle in the middle of Chloe's room. Light snow flutters to the ground outside as the inside heater pushes to keep up with the cold. I have spent the last half hour catching up with Chloe and Eric. We cover the basic topics of school, college, summer memories, and how we are doing. It's just like old times, except someone is missing.

"It's been a while since we actually saw you in person, Butler." Eric grins.

"Have you looked outside? I'm pretty sure last time I was here, we were all wearing shorts," I joke, trying to disguise my strong dislike of the weather outside.

Chloe gets up and walks over to the window. "Man, Marc should have been here a half hour ago..." she mutters as she returns to sit with us.

"He's actually here?" I ask, my stomach fluttering with sudden excitement. "He told me he thought he would be out here for the holidays, but I haven't seen him."

"Well, when you showed up, all three of us were going to be here to surprise you, but obviously that isn't happening..." Chloe says, sounding annoyed.

"Marc's never late, is he?" I ask, already knowing the answer.

Chloe shakes her head. "I don't know where he is."

"So, how's he been?"

"I've only seen him a couple of times, so ask Eric. He sees him every day." Chloe pulls her blonde hair into a ponytail.

"He's good," Eric replies. "At least now..."

"What do you mean?"

"You see, right after his accident he wasn't really himself. He was upset a lot of the time because he couldn't do the stuff he loved. He also hated asking for help and tried to distance himself from us the best he could. He's all healed now and good as new. He's basically his old self again. A lot quieter though," Eric says, stretching his legs out.

"Quieter?" I ask.

"Yeah, I think the whole 'I'm severely injured' thing was a humbling experience for him," Chloe says. "Not to mention he isn't into driving full speed anymore or crazy stuff like that, but he's still Marc."

"Have you not talked to him?" Eric asks.

"No, I have...at least in texts and emails, but until recently he has seemed really distant. He'd always just want to hear about me, or if he did reply to one of my questions, it was always a vague response."

"Sounds about right," Eric says. "He's just getting back into the routine of being perfectly healed. In the last month, his attitude has improved. He's become more optimistic."

I stand up and go look out the window. "He has?"

"Yeah, and I know he is really looking forward to seeing you."

I slowly nod.

"Why do you look so surprised?" Eric asks. "I just talked to him about this yesterday."

"Well, then why did Marc just walk up to the front door only to turn around and walk away?"

"What?" Eric stands up and joins me at the window. Chloe does as well. The three of us watch Marc, in his hat, jacket, and boots, trudge out of the driveway onto the road.

"What the heck is he doing?" Chloe asks.

"Maybe he forgot something?" Eric suggests.

"I'll go find out," I say.

"In the cold?" Chloe asks. "I would freeze, and I live here during the winter."

"I'll be fine. I want to talk to Marc, and if Marc doesn't want to come here, I'll go to him."

"Okay." Chloe smiles.

"Don't freeze, Butler." Eric chuckles as I walk out into the hall.

⸻ «◉» ⸻

I'm only outside for two minutes when the deep cold reaches me, making me shiver, even with all my snow gear on. I look down at the driveway to see if I can see the footprints of where Marc would have gone, but since all the neighbors come and go all the time, I can't make out which set of prints is his.

I walk around the back of the house, toward the lake, to see if Marc went to the ice- covered water when we looked away from the window, but I have no luck seeing him. I end up heading back to the main road and in the direction of his house. Maybe he went home to get something. Or maybe he just didn't feel like being social.

I breathe the cool air in slowly, watching my icy breath appear as I exhale. I walk quickly, even though the snow-packed forest is pretty.

"Although I love the lake and the sun during summer, there is something about the icicles and snow that makes this place a whole lot calmer in the winter," a voice says behind me. "But something tells me you really dislike the cold..."

I stop walking. "Marc?"

When I get no reply, I turn around. He stands not far behind me. Like me, he wears jeans, mittens, and snow boots, but compared to my large parka, his ski shell looks slim and light. He wears a knit hat, and his golden-brown bangs fall out the front. His deep blue eyes seem alive and full of life, unlike the last time I saw him. A modest smile forms across his face.

"Aren't you cold?" I ask, for it is the only thing I can think to say.

He shakes his head. "You get used to it," he shrugs, "especially after all these years."

"What are you doing out here?"

"Walking. It clears my mind. Plus, I didn't think I was ready to face you at Chloe's..."

"Face me? What do you mean?"

"Do you want to go on a little walk with me?"

"If you don't mind," I reply.

"Unless you don't think you can handle the cool air."

I quietly laugh and I can see my icy breath. "No, I'll be fine. Besides, it's really pretty out here."

"I know," he replies, looking up at the long tree branches intertwined and covered with snow above us. Snowflakes begin to fall, and I stick my tongue out to catch them.

"Have you ever listened to the snow fall?" Marc asks.

"Listened?" I say, slightly confused.

"Many people claim you can't hear anything, but I think they're wrong." He pauses. "Here, don't move, and just listen for a minute."

I do what he says. "What exactly am I going to hear?" I say after some time.

"That's the thing," he replies. "I like the sound of the small icy flakes floating. You can't really hear them. You just hear the empty air around you. It is as if everything is still and unmoving."

"I like it," I reply, smiling.

Marc starts walking, his boots crunching through the snow. He is silent. I follow him. The silence drags on and our conversation is going nowhere fast. "All right, Marc," I finally say. "We aren't strangers."

"I know," he softly replies.

"Why aren't you ready to 'face me'?"

"I feel bad. Even though we have kept in touch, I feel like I have distanced myself from you..."

"You had a lot going on. It was only natural."

He cuts me off. "You don't need to defend me, Aly. I'm sorry for my lack of communication. I tried to shut everyone out. Don't take it personally. I just feel bad because all your emails were so detailed and kind, and mine were all detached, concrete responses."

"Your letter wasn't," I say, looking at him.

"Letter?"

"The one you wrote to me as your good-bye."

"You got that?" he asks, looking somewhat shocked.

I nod. "With the clever eyes of Matt."

A smile forms on his face. "I thought it would have been lost in the crash..."

"It wasn't." I smile back at him. "You're welcome, Marc."

He just nods.

"So how are you doing?" I ask. "Honestly?"

He sighs. "Now, I'm great, but if you would have asked me two months ago, I would have had a completely different answer. My leg was broken, I had stitches all over my body, my car was destroyed, I couldn't play basketball, someone really close to me had just died, and you were gone. Let's just say the beginning of the school year was a low point.

"But then things got better. I was able to help coach the pre-season practices and tryouts, and once I got a boot, I could actually practice shooting. The season starts in January and my doctor says I can play, so I'm really looking forward to that. After all, I'm a captain."

"That's good," I say as our boots crunch through the snow.

"I was really upset about...well...everything for a while, but then I started thinking. I just needed to make the best of the situation. So I tried. Now my car is all fixed, and I'm all healed, except for a couple of scars."

"Glad to hear. So...um...how's driving?" I ask, not really sure how to state my question kindly. "You stopped your habit of speeding, right?"

He nods, chuckling. "I gave that up months ago and learned to channel stress into other, safer activities. I'm not going through another accident again. In fact, I'm pretty sure I drive below the speed limit most of the time now."

"It's better than above," I say.

We grow silent again. I look down the familiar road. Just months ago, it was so filled with life, all green—now it is so white and cold.

"How have you been?" he asks me.

"Well, I'm happy to report that I haven't snuck out, stolen money from anyone, and the parties I do go to are the ones my parents know about. I have been applying to colleges, and shocker: my parents and I kind of get along now."

"I knew it would all work out," he says, elbowing me.

"Well, it's mostly because of you," I say, looking into his deep blue eyes.

"Me? Aly, I already told you in my letter, I was just there to help you as you helped yourself."

"But if you hadn't tried so hard to be my friend, my whole summer up here would have sucked, and I would have never tried to change my behaviors."

He looks at me like I am joking.

"I'm not lying!" I say in a serious voice. "The first day I actually talked to you, you 'read me,' and that description you gave me really frightened me because that wasn't who I wanted to be. I didn't want to be some snobby, rich, popular girl. You helped put it in perspective, Marc, you really did."

"I guess we both helped each other in our own ways. You're coming back next summer, right?"

"You don't even have to ask. I wouldn't miss it for the world. Everything is so perfect up here."

"It's a great place," he says.

"Promise me we will always keep in touch..."

"Promise," he replies. "And I promise I will reply to you in more detail."

I laugh. "Sounds good...and thank you for tolerating me those first few days I was here. I really needed a friend."

"Well, what are friends for?"

I lean toward him and him toward me, and then our lips meet. I wrap my hands around his neck. I feel the warmth of his body close to mine, and as we kiss, my heart flutters. We slowly break away and he looks at me.

"I thought you were afraid of long-distance relationships."

I smile. "I thought you were afraid of possible rejection."

We fall silent again. The snow falls, and our boots crunch through it as we begin to walk again, hand in hand. A bird calls overhead. I glance over at Marc, one of the only people I can call a real friend. He was the first person to trust me again, the first person to really try to help me. The two of us continue walking through the canopy of trees, and for once in my life everything is perfect.

"Marc?" I finally say, choosing my words carefully.

"Yeah, Aly?"

"Thank you."

"What are you thanking me for this time?" he asks.

"Thank you for taking me on a ride last summer."

He smiles and so do I.

THE BEGINNING

CPSIA information can be obtained
at www.ICGtesting.com
Printed in the USA
FSHW021539310719
60571FS